A Christmas in Shady Springs

Shady Springs Book Three

Sarah Anne Crouch

Scrivenings PRESS
Quench your thirst for story.
www.ScriveningsPress.com

Published by Scrivenings Press LLC
15 Lucky Lane
Morrilton, Arkansas 72110
https://ScriveningsPress.com

Printed in the United States of America

Paperback ISBN 978-1-64917-545-8

eBook ISBN 978-1-64917-546-5

Editors: Amy R. Anguish and Kathy McKinsey

Cover design by Sarah Anne Crouch and Linda Fulkerson

Scripture quotations are from the ESV Bible® (The Holy Bible, English Standard Version®), copyright © 2001 by Crossway Bibles, a publishing ministry of Good News Publishers. Used by permission. All rights reserved.

All characters are fictional, and any resemblance to real people, either factual or historical, is purely coincidental.

OCTOBER

*M*adeleine Mullins's perfect wedding would be like a fairy tale. She'd float down the aisle in a gorgeous white dress—beautiful but tasteful. Her hair would be done half up with curls cascading down her back. Guests would be surrounded by flowers, soft light, and soaring music. Closing her eyes, she could picture the affair down to the last detail.

But nothing she'd previously imagined or planned could have prepared her for her actual wedding.

"I finished the invitations. Come see." Madeleine tugged her fiancé's arm, pulling him into her aunt's kitchen.

She might never get over how nice A.J.'s arms felt under her fingers. Years of sports along with his current job as a track coach and church handyman led to a lean, muscular build. The smile he flashed her way wasn't so bad, either.

"Okay, okay. I'm coming."

Aunt Clara's kitchen was flooded with bright morning light, highlighting the box sitting out on the table. Lifting the first invitation, she held it up.

"What do you think?"

She'd spent every spare moment of the last week painting

each invitation by hand. A watercolor spray of flowers in burgundy and forest green circled the calligraphy swirling across the center. Their names—Madeleine Mullins and A.J. Young—danced in curled letters.

"It's perfect." A.J. grinned as he took the square of cardstock from her hands and held it up to the sunlight. His auburn hair glowed in the rays streaming through the kitchen windows, and his green eyes sparkled as he turned his gaze to her. "I can't believe how great these turned out."

He kissed her on the cheek, then handed back the card. "What do *you* think?"

"I love them." Gazing at the creamy white paper, her smile matched his. She'd spent many long nights agonizing over the design of these wedding invitations. And all that work had paid off.

"This wedding is a reflection of us." Madeleine lovingly placed the card back with the others. She lifted the lid over the top and slowly slid it down. "It's the first day of our marriage. And I want everything to be perfect and beautiful."

"But what happens when something goes wrong?"

Madeleine paused for a beat. "It won't." She stroked the lid of the invitations box. "We're going to have the perfect wedding."

A.J. took Madeleine's hands and lifted them to his lips. He kissed the tips of her fingers before pulling her into his arms. "I want it to be perfect for you. But I worry about you." He hugged her tight, his chin resting on her head. "I don't want you to stress so much about every little detail."

"I'm an artist. That's what I do." Madeleine's arms circled A.J.'s waist. She deeply breathed in the smell of him. Even though it was only soap and laundry detergent, his unique scent always sent a thrill through her. Her heart rate slowed to a steady beat.

"Well, Madeleine Mullins, famous artist, you also agreed to

marry a poor school teacher and aspiring grad-student." He pulled back to look at her face. "With only about two and a half months to plan the wedding."

"Two months now."

"Even worse." He cupped her cheeks in his hands. "So please give yourself some grace. It's all going to be okay. As long as we end up married at the end of that day, the rest is just icing on the cake."

"I know it will be." If each detail fell into place exactly right, they'd have a beautiful wedding signifying a beautiful marriage. The invitations were only the beginning.

After everything they'd been through together, Madeleine's rocky faith journey, a broken engagement, and a rushed wedding, Madeleine *needed* their special day to be perfect.

"I'll do everything I can to make that happen for you. I promise." He stepped back. "And this weekend, that means meeting with Sam and Mr. Patterson about the plans for the ceremony."

"I wish I could go with you." Madeleine grimaced. Now that the invitations were complete, she had to address one hundred envelopes. But before that, she had an appointment with the florist and a phone call with the caterer.

"Divide and conquer." A.J. gave her one last kiss before pulling his jacket from the hall coat rack and opening the front door. "I love you. Don't worry."

"I love you too."

If he only knew how much work was still left to be done, he'd probably be as stressed as she was.

2

———————————

"You can't have the wedding on Christmas Eve."

"Pardon?" A.J. couldn't trust his ears. Surely he'd heard wrong.

"You can't possibly have the wedding on December twenty-fourth." John Patterson, one of the church elders, stared back at him from across the room. His face was set in a scowl, but A.J. had a hard time taking him seriously when he wore a T-shirt that read *This is my corny costume* with giant candy corn on it.

The room was small, so their knees were practically touching. Sam Sullivan, the longtime preacher at Shady Springs Church, had an office about the size of a walk-in closet. But with all of the books lining every wall, it felt more like a cupboard. Somehow, Sam also managed to fit a large desk, a couple chairs, and several stacks of papers.

A clock ticked on the wall, marking passing seconds.

"But we already have the invitations. Madeleine hand painted each one." A.J. looked back and forth between Mr. Patterson and Sam, hoping one of them could clear this situation right up. "Clara checked the calendar as soon as we started planning the wedding."

"Well, I don't know which calendar she checked, but she never asked me." Mr. Patterson cleared his throat. "I would've told her we have the Christmas pageant that night."

Of course. For a while, Shady Springs had skipped the annual nativity play. People were too busy or they couldn't find enough children to participate. But this year, the parents had asked to bring it back. He'd seen the announcements about planning meetings and play practice—he just hadn't realized what day the performance would be.

"The pageant is on Christmas Eve?"

Mr. Patterson looked at him like he'd lost his mind. "Of course, it is. When else would we have it? Halloween?"

He wasn't opposed, although that might be a little soon, considering it was already October twenty-ninth.

Sam sighed. "We can't reschedule Christmas. Not even for you and Maddy."

"I mean, Jesus almost certainly wasn't born in December ..." A.J. let the rest of his sentence trail off. Mr. Patterson and Sam were clearly not amused.

"Okay." A.J. bounced his knees, racking his brain for ideas. Going back to Madeleine with this information was simply not an option. "Could we have the wedding in a different part of the building? Maybe we could use the fellowship hall while the pageant is going on in the auditorium."

Sam and Mr. Patterson shared a look with one another before answering him.

"You don't want that." Sam winced.

"Weddings are chaos. Add a host of small children in costumes? Plus the live animals we'll have in the parking lot?" Mr. Patterson shook his head. "No, you don't want that."

He hadn't heard about the live animals. That might cause a bit of a traffic jam for their wedding guests.

"Okay, then what do you suggest I tell Maddy?"

Sam flipped through the calendar in front of him. Yes, the church still used a paper calendar and not digital.

"We're supposed to host our missionaries from Honduras on December eighteenth. And there's rehearsals for the Christmas play." He tapped a date on the page. "How about December seventeenth? It's the Saturday before."

A.J. leaned forward to look at the day Sam suggested. There was something written down already. "That's the day of the cookie decorating and caroling."

Every year, some of the older ladies from the congregation baked several dozen sugar cookies, people donated frosting and sprinkles, and all the kids and their parents came out to decorate cookies before delivering them to the nursing home and singing carols. It was a much-loved annual event, and everyone would be upset if it didn't happen.

"I'm sure we can move that around," Sam said. "I'm trying to help you out here." He turned to Mr. Patterson, eyebrows raised.

"I'll talk to the parents and see what they say." Mr. Patterson folded his arms so that only the tops of the candy corn on his shirt showed. "But we have a bigger problem than that right now."

What could possibly be bigger than rescheduling the entire wedding? After invitations had already been made?

"In order to get married here, you have to complete premarital counseling."

A.J. sighed in relief. "That's not a problem. Maddy and I were already planning to meet with Sam for counseling." He turned to the preacher. "If that's okay with you. I know we haven't set up any sessions yet, but I figured we'd have plenty of time between now and the wedding."

"I'd be happy to walk you through the workbook I've used in the past, but..." Sam trailed off, waving his left hand with its empty ring finger. "I've never been married. Because of that, I like to ask engaged couples I counsel to also interview a variety of married couples in order to get a perspective I'm not able to provide."

"That makes sense." A.J. had confidence they'd find enough married people willing to help them out. After all, it seemed like all his friends from high school and college got married ages ago. "I don't think that'll be an issue."

"Okay. If you promise to complete your premarital counseling, we can move forward with the new date for the wedding." Mr. Patterson rocked forward in his seat.

But they already *had* a date for the wedding—Christmas Eve. It was all Madeleine wanted. And all *he* wanted was to get married without causing his bride to hate him before they even walked the aisle. Why couldn't people compromise a little? Who said a Christmas play had to be in December?

He turned to Sam, mentally pleading for some assistance.

Sam set both hands on his desk, his fingers splayed. "Let's agree to wait to send those invitations until we find a solution."

Giving a quick nod, A.J. stood. "I just wish one of you would volunteer to tell Madeleine the news for me."

Mr. Patterson laughed good naturedly as he walked out of the office. But A.J. didn't find any of this funny.

3

"Is that all of them?" Madeleine scanned the envelopes and people spread all over her aunt's living room. Her dad and A.J. would've stayed to help today, but they were busy with their own projects. Dad with his work as a portrait photographer and A.J. with finalizing details on the wedding venue. As it turned out, Madeleine was grateful for the time spent with some of her favorite ladies.

"Let's gather everything up and double-check." Her mom Catherine spoke with an authoritative air, although Madeleine knew she was anxious about the wedding happening in only two months. She'd mentioned as much only a few dozen times.

Planning a Christmas wedding on such short notice was a daunting task, but if anyone could pull it off, these women could. Her Aunt Clara had held the family together through triumphs and tragedies—the loss of her husband, the separation and reunification of Madeleine's parents, and Madeleine's own journey back to Christ. Every time Clara had been there to soften the blows and lift everyone up. She never shied away from the truth but spoke it with grace and love.

Nancy Jones had been a friend of the family for a long time. Well, except for several years when Madeleine basically hated her and blamed her for her mother's leaving Shady Springs. But now all was forgiven and the past was water under the bridge. Nancy had been like a mother to Madeleine's dad and was making up for lost time.

"Thank you all so much for helping me. I was dreading addressing all of the wedding invitations by myself." Madeleine threw an arm around Aunt Clara who hugged her back.

"Of course, sweetheart. We're happy to help out." Clara squeezed Madeleine around the waist with one arm, practically lifting her off the floor in her exuberance.

"That's all of them." Mom started to hand Madeleine the envelopes but pulled back. "Actually, let me mail these for you. I have to run by the grocery store and the post office is right around the corner."

"If you're sure, I would love that." One less item on her list was a win. She sighed contentedly as she smoothed the fabric of her jeans. "I think we may actually pull this off." Madeleine beamed, looking at the other women.

"We'll see." Mom raised her eyebrows but smiled as she took the invitations and walked out the front door

Ding.

Madeleine saw a text alert on her phone from A.J.

Where are you right now?

She typed a quick reply before sliding her phone in her back pocket.

"What's next on your list?" Clara walked around the living room with a wastebasket, picking up little peel-off sticker backings from the envelopes.

"We have to order dresses for bridesmaids and suits for the groomsmen." Madeleine massaged her temples and plopped back down on the sofa. "Honestly, I almost want to have everyone just wear an outfit they already own."

"Why not do that?" Clara popped her head up, eyes wide.

"Sounds like a great idea to me." Nancy spoke up from the armchair in the corner.

Waving her hands dismissively, Madeleine frowned. "No, no. How would that look with everyone up front in completely different outfits? Even if I told everyone to wear maroon or something, there's bound to be all different shades of red." She shivered at the thought.

"Weddings used to be very different." Nancy tilted her head, her gaze wandering to the wall across from her. "There's too much pressure on young people now to have a picture-perfect ceremony."

Madeleine followed Nancy's line of vision. The wall was filled with family photos, many of which featured her Uncle George. And right in the middle was a wedding picture. Clara wore a simple gown with capped sleeves and nary a train to speak of. Instead of an elaborate veil, her head was adorned with a flowered headband. Madeleine didn't remember the ceremony—she was too young—but she grinned from her mother's arms. The seven of them, Madeleine, her parents, Clara, George, and Madeleine's grandparents, all looked radiant.

"My wedding was very small," Clara said. Only family and a few close friends. But it was the happiest day of my life."

"Would you change anything about it?" Madeleine scooted forward, watching her aunt's face. The hint of a wistful smile tugged at Clara's lips.

"Oh, sure. Lots of things went wrong." She gave a short laugh. "The cake was dry and the musicians were off-key. But …" Clara trailed off and tore her gaze from the wedding photo to look at Madeleine. "No, actually. I don't think I'd change a thing."

Clara carried the wastebasket to the next room. Madeleine turned to Nancy.

"What about you, Nancy? Would you change anything from your wedding?"

"Not much." Nancy twisted her wedding ring. "I wish we'd taken more pictures."

"Well, I've got that part covered." Madeleine's dad Henry had agreed to document her wedding day with the help of his assistant.

She sat back. After a beat, she said, "I hope I can be like you and Clara. No regrets. Just beautiful memories of a perfect day."

"It wasn't perfect by any means."

Madeleine shrugged. "You know what I mean. I want a wedding that I can look back on fondly." She gazed down at her engagement ring A.J. had done such a good job choosing. A brilliant sapphire sat between two small diamonds in a vintage-inspired setting. It was beautiful without being over-the-top. Modest but enchanting. "I want a wedding that feels like us and celebrates our love." Madeleine grimaced. "That sounded really cheesy."

"No, I understand." Clara smiled as she entered the room. "I think every bride wants that, but then you get to the day and realize …" She shrugged and looked to Nancy, seemingly searching for the right words.

"None of it matters as much as you thought it did."

A knock sounded at the front door.

"I'll go get that." Clara left and Madeleine heard A.J.'s voice coming from the front hall.

"Is Maddy here?" The sound of footsteps grew nearer.

Madeleine turned just as A.J. entered the room. Her stomach clenched at the expression on his face. Something was wrong. He'd been in a meeting with one of the elders and their officiant, Sam, to discuss wedding details and using the church building. It was supposed to be very straightforward.

"What is it?" Her voice raised in pitch.

A.J. took a deep breath. Seeing him out-of-sorts amped up her anxiety. He never worried about small stuff, so whatever was bothering him must be big.

"They won't let us use the church building on Christmas Eve."

No. A tight ball of anxiety formed in her chest, and her lungs stopped cooperating.

Deep breaths, Madeleine.

"What?" Clara stood behind A.J., her mouth hanging slightly open. "But I asked Sam to put it on the calendar."

"We forgot about the Christmas pageant."

Her stomach dropped. A sickening chill crept over her. *Of course.* How had she not put two and two together? She sucked in another breath.

"You're right." Clara ran a hand through her short hair. "But why wasn't it on the church calendar?"

A.J. shrugged. "Probably no one thought to put it on."

Nancy let out a *hmm* from the corner.

Madeleine gasped. "Wait."

Clara turned to her at the same time, a panicked expression on her face.

"The invitations."

"I know," A.J. held his hands out. "I told them the invitations had been made already."

"No." Madeleine grabbed her phone from her back pocket. No time for a text. She punched her mom's contact on her phone.

She shook out her right hand as she paced the floor, clutching the phone with her left. "Come on, Mom. Answer, answer." She inhaled slowly through her nostrils, but her heart still raced.

When voicemail clicked on, she hung up. Three pairs of eyes watched her from across the room.

"Well?" Clara asked, wringing her hands.

"She didn't answer. I'll text her to call me back right away."

"Tell her it's an emergency." Nancy's voice was shrill. "Oh, dear."

Clara rubbed Nancy's shoulder comfortingly.

"What's going on? What's wrong?" A.J. turned back and forth between the women in the room, obviously startled by everyone's reaction.

"Mom is at the post office mailing the invitations right now."

"Let's go catch her. We can take my car." A.J. clasped Madeleine around the waist, steadying her. Finally, the calm-and-collected A.J. had returned.

Madeleine's phone rang, and she tossed it in surprise, nearly dropping it on the floor. A.J. caught it right before it landed, handing it to Madeleine.

"Mom?"

"What is it, sweetie? What's wrong?" The sound blared from Madeleine's phone. She must've hit a button and put her mom on speaker.

"Did you mail the invitations?"

"I thought you said this was an emergency."

"Mom!" Madeleine growled in frustration.

"Yes, I mailed the invitations." Mom matched her aggravated tone of voice. "I don't know why you don't trust me to—"

"Go back!" Several shouts joined hers from the others in the living room. "Mom, we can't mail the invitations. The date is wrong."

"What? No it isn't. December—"

"Just trust me. We have to get those invitations back."

"Okay, okay. I'll call you later."

Madeleine sank to the couch.

"I think we should still go to the post office, just in case." A.J. held out a hand, and Madeleine took it, letting him pull her back to standing.

While they were on the road, Mom called again. "They won't

let me get the invitations back because my name isn't on the envelopes."

"Okay, A.J. and I are on our way."

"Hurry, the post office is closing soon."

They were only five minutes away. Madeleine wasn't worried about making it on time. She was worried about what would happen when they arrived.

4

As soon as A.J. put his car in park, Madeleine flung open her door and raced inside. "I'm here!"

An unsmiling postal worker stared back at her from behind a counter.

"This is my daughter." Mom pointed a finger. "See? And her fiancé." A.J. followed quickly behind.

"Can we please have our wedding invitations back?" Madeleine clasped her hands together, squeezing tightly.

"May I see your driver's licenses?" The postal worker—Bill, if his nametag was to be believed—held out a hand flicking his fingers toward himself.

"Sure." A.J. pulled out his wallet and Madeleine did the same.

Bill examined their IDs, turning them over. "Okay." He handed the cards back to them and turned to the wall behind him, opening a drawer. "If you'll fill out this form, you can file a Mail Recall."

Madeleine's blood pressure skyrocketed. And from the looks of it, her mother was feeling the same.

"Bill. Can I call you Bill?" A.J. stepped up to the counter. "We've made a terrible mistake."

Bill frowned, unimpressed.

"Are you married, Bill?"

Reluctantly, Bill grunted in assent.

"We've been working very hard to plan a wedding for this Christmas." A.J. reached behind him, and Madeleine squeezed his hand. He pulled her close. "And we've just been told by the church that we can't have our wedding on the date we'd planned."

Although Bill didn't let go of the Mail Recall form, his frown smoothed out.

"I'm just trying to help my bride have her dream wedding. And we can't have our dream wedding if the invitations are incorrect."

Bill sighed deeply. Obviously, this conversation pained him greatly. "I'll see if the invitations are still here."

Madeleine buried her head in A.J.'s shoulder as Bill walked through a side door. Sobs welled in her chest, aching to break free. Even if they retrieved the invitations, what then? Could they still have a wedding at the church building? Two months out was too late to book any decent wedding venues. And they hadn't budgeted for anything more expensive. Which is to say, more than free.

Stroking her hair with one hand, and holding her tight with the other, A.J. swayed back and forth. "It's going to be okay."

As much as she could while pressed against his shoulder, Madeleine nodded her head. The only good thing about wedding planning was how it had brought them closer together. Trauma bonding, or something like that.

At long last, Bill returned, although the ticking clock on the wall insisted only minutes had passed.

"Is this them?"

"Yes!" Mom popped up from leaning against the wall.

They all raced to the counter to check the envelopes. Of course, what they knew about Bill's fastidious commitment to the rules and regulations of the US Postal system should've told them he never would've returned with the wrong invitations.

Relief washed over her as Madeleine picked up the stack of envelopes with her and A.J.'s names stamped across the back. "These are the ones."

"Thank you, Bill." A.J. reached across the counter for a hearty handshake and, surprisingly, Bill obliged. "You've saved the day."

Bill shrugged, but the corner of his mouth lifted in what was probably a smile.

"Thank you, Bill!" Madeleine clutched the invitations to her chest, choosing to take the win and ignore, for the moment, how they still had a giant problem.

Madeleine held a stack of beautiful wedding invitations. Artistically designed, hand addressed with love, stamped invitations … with the wrong date.

* * *

"But when are we going to get married?" Madeleine sat across from A.J. at Aunt Clara's kitchen table.

Nancy had gone home after they'd shared the story of getting the invitations back from the clutches of Bill and the post office. Madeleine couldn't possibly ask her to stay and stuff envelopes. *Again.* Even if Nancy did offer, she seemed tired from the first round of sending out wedding invitations.

A.J.'s chest moved up and down as he breathed deeply. "They suggested the Saturday before. December seventeenth."

She sat straight. "But that's not Christmas Eve."

"I think that was the point."

There were many reasons she wanted to get married on Christmas Eve. Family and friends would be off for the holidays, but only very close family and friends would actually show up for a holiday wedding. She'd figured they could invite lots of people and only expect a small number to come.

She and A.J. would always be able to remember their wedding anniversary, and they could celebrate anytime they wanted around the holiday season.

And a final reason that wasn't logical, but that she couldn't ignore, a Christmas Eve wedding was so *romantic*. The poetry of it spoke to her heart.

December seventeenth. She mulled over the new date in her head.

"December seventeenth." She tested out the feel of it in her mouth.

A.J. lifted a brow.

A deep sigh escaped her chest. "Okay."

Aunt Clara and Mom joined them with mugs of tea. "What do you want to do now?"

"We don't have time to print new invitations." They'd lost a week of planning time in one day. "We're already running behind. People usually expect wedding invitations two months in advance."

A.J. gave a dry laugh. "We barely got that much time ourselves."

"True." Mom smirked before taking a sip of her chamomile tea.

"You'll need new envelopes, right?" Clara turned over one of the invitations in her hands. "Unless we want to try to steam them open and reseal them."

"And then sneak them past Bill somehow." Madeleine laughed.

"I can drive to the store to buy more envelopes," A.J. volunteered. "I don't mind. And I can pick up some food for tonight."

"Good idea. I'll put a list together." Clara bounced up to grab a notebook and pen from the kitchen.

"But what about the date?" Mom asked. Her voice was quiet.

Madeleine knew her mom understood how much she'd agonized over those invitations. Mom had to sit through every complaint, cast votes on design options like it was a national election, and then smile politely when Madeleine ignored all her input and picked something completely different anyway.

She let her shoulders slump and her head fall forward. "We'll mark out the old date and write the new one in."

Rubbing her shoulders, Mom leaned in. "I'm proud of you. I know how hard you worked. And it will still be beautiful."

Nodding, Madeleine stood up. "Can you and Clara do it? I can't watch."

"Sure, we'll let you know when the envelopes are ready."

Madeleine slumped up to her bedroom. She wouldn't pout for long—there was too much work to do. But sometimes it was nice to stop being an adult for a minute and let your mom take care of you.

* * *

"Knock, knock." Aunt Clara poked her head in the room. "A.J. is back and the envelopes are ready to be addressed. Your dad will be here soon to help out."

"Thank you, Aunt Clara." Madeleine closed her notebook. She'd picked it up to work through her wedding checklist, but ended up sketching instead.

"You okay? I know today was a whirlwind."

"I was upset about the invitations—and the wedding date—but I'll be okay." She slid the notebook to the top of the desk, then swiveled in her chair, wrapping her fingers around the wooden back. "Actually, I have something else I'm worried about right now."

"What is it, sweetie?" Clara perched on the bed.

Madeleine scrunched up her face. She knew she needed advice, but wasn't sure how to ask. "I don't—" She looked up at the white ceiling for a moment. Deep breath. "I don't know who to ask to walk me down the aisle."

Her statement hung in the air while Clara digested the information.

"Wow." Clara sat back against the pillows. "I hadn't really thought about that."

"I mean, my parents are back together and things are going really well, but …" She flapped her hands. Clara knew everything her family had been through over the years.

"But Henry walked out on you and your mom when you were a child. And wasn't a real father to you for most of your life."

Bingo. Madeleine had worked hard, really hard, to rebuild a relationship with her dad. But would they ever get to the place they were before he left? When she was young? She couldn't know at this point. She'd forgiven him, but forgiveness didn't magically repair all the hurt overnight.

And Mom. They'd been through so much together. Mom was her best friend.

"Why not have your mom walk you down the aisle?"

"I thought about that," Madeleine said. "And that was my plan when I dreamed about getting married years ago. But, now they're back together and what if I hurt Dad's feelings? Or Mom's feelings?"

"Have you talked to your mom about this?"

Madeleine shook her head. "I'm afraid of offending her either way."

"Hmm." Clara ran her hand over the quilt. "But what do *you* want? Who do you want to give you away?"

"Could I just give myself away?"

Clara chuckled. "I guess. It's not like there are any rules. God didn't give us the ten commandments of wedding ceremonies."

Madeleine rested her forehead against the chair back. "I don't mind having a traditional wedding ceremony. And I like the symbolism of starting a new family with A.J." She lifted her head again to look at her aunt. "I wish I had a normal family."

"Sorry, kiddo." Clara waggled her eyebrows. "We're all a little weird here. I'm surprised you're not used to it by now."

Madeleine rose from the chair to leave, but Clara tugged her onto the bed. "You don't have to decide what you want to do today. But let me pray over you right now."

The gentle words of Aunt Clara's prayer washed over her, and Madeleine relaxed into her aunt's side. God had brought her family through ups and downs, and He wasn't going to leave her side anytime soon.

5

For four years, A.J. had opened up the church building in Shady Springs every Sunday as the caretaker/part-time youth minister/handyman. He was going to miss the quiet ritual of unlocking the doors, checking the thermostat, and warming up the projector. In less than a year, he'd be leaving Shady Springs for grad school and a new phase of life.

He and Madeleine hadn't found a home yet. They'd done a few internet searches, but wedding planning had taken up most of Madeleine's mental energy. Nevertheless, he imagined them in a small space somewhere close to campus. They'd find a new church to worship with temporarily. He hoped it would be a small congregation, just like Shady Springs.

As A.J. flipped on the lights in the auditorium, he reminisced about the years he'd spent in the room. Sermons, singings, Vacation Bible School, youth group activities. He'd set up a relay for the teens climbing over these very pews not too long ago. And they'd had a Nerf gun fight the year before. There was still a mark on one of the walls from that night. His good intentions to paint over kept slipping his mind.

The people here had opened their hearts to him—and Madeleine—allowing them into their lives and showering them with love and generosity. Leaving the church in Shady Springs was the hardest part of the decision to move away for grad school.

It helped that he knew they'd be coming back to visit Madeleine's Aunt Clara. And he knew everyone here was proud of his decision to become a full-time minister. He'd enjoyed his last four years teaching at Shady Springs High School while working part-time for the church, but the time had come to pursue his dreams. The world of education was fulfilling, but not his true calling. The decision to leave Shady Springs stirred up a swirl of anxiety and sadness, but the countless prayers he'd lifted up to God gave him a sense of peace. He knew he was making the right move.

"Good morning." Sam stepped in through the double-doors of the auditorium. He scanned the room until he found A.J. in the audio/visual booth—a raised space at the back with a sound panel and a computer.

"Hey, Sam. Looking forward to your sermon this morning. The slides are up and running." A.J. clicked through Sam's PowerPoint, the images showing up on the screens at the front of the auditorium. He muted the screen and scrolled back to the opening slide for the worship service.

"Thanks." Sam stepped into the booth and placed a hand on his shoulder. "How did Madeleine take the news?"

A.J. glanced up from the computer. Sam's eyes shone with concern.

"It wasn't great. The invitations had already gone out."

Sam's eyebrows shot up and his hand tightened on A.J's shoulder.

"Don't worry, we got them back." He patted Sam's arm as the man breathed a sigh of relief.

"Did you suggest the new date to her?"

"Yeees." He dragged the word out. "She wasn't thrilled, but I guess it's our only option. So, we changed the date on the invitations. We'll send them all out again on Monday."

"Good. We'll make sure to get the wedding on the calendar this time." Sam moved to head out the door, but stopped himself. "Let's set up a time to meet for counseling. Talk to Maddy and let me know what works for you. December will be here before we know it."

Seriously.

It wasn't until after church services were over that A.J. finally got a quiet moment to talk to Madeleine. He tugged on her hand as the rest of the people in the auditorium moseyed toward the exit.

"I talked to Sam this morning."

She smiled up at him, her face framed by golden brown hair. Often when Maddy was painting or working, she'd pull her hair back in a bun or ponytail. But always on Sundays, she wore it down, and he loved it so much it drove him crazy. He ran his free hand through her soft curls just because he could.

"What about?"

"He wants to start our premarital counseling sessions. And I think he feels bad making us move the wedding date."

Maddy rolled her neck to one side, rubbing her shoulder. "It's not his fault we forgot about the Christmas pageant." She sighed, stretching her neck in the other direction. "I'm just overwhelmed with wedding details. We have to send those invites out as soon as possible. We're already behind schedule."

"You're right. We can't have a wedding without inviting anyone." He narrowed his eyes in thought, turning his hand until their fingers intertwined. "Or could we? I mean, I'm not entirely opposed to running off just the two of us."

Maddy's laugh was genuine this time. "Stop it."

He pulled her close. "What do you say? A nice quiet ceremony? You, me, the courthouse judge?"

"Don't be ridiculous. Our moms would kill us." She raised one eyebrow, smirking at him.

"You have a point there." Not to mention the dozen church ladies who told him every time they saw him how happy they were he'd finally found someone to marry and how much they were looking forward to the wedding. "It would be a tragic way to go."

"Right. And I want a nice, long life with you."

"Me too." He gave her a hug. Nothing like the long embrace he wished for. Those church ladies might be looking forward to the wedding, but they wouldn't be happy with him making out with his future bride in the middle of the auditorium.

* * *

After setting up their first counseling session with Sam for that afternoon—even though Madeleine had countered with a dozen other things she needed to be working on—a middle-aged woman in a navy-blue dress cornered them. "John told me about the wedding date." She shook her head and widened her eyes in a sympathetic expression.

"Thanks, Susan." For whatever reason, A.J. always felt more comfortable calling Mrs. Patterson by her first name and her husband by his last name.

"I'm sorry, dear." Susan barely looked at him, pulling both of Madeleine's hands into hers. "I hate that we couldn't have the wedding on the date you wanted." She gave a sad pout.

"Thank you." Madeleine's shoulders relaxed.

"Listen, if we can help in any way—"

"Actually," A.J. interrupted. "There is something we need help with."

Madeleine and Susan both looked at him with curious expressions.

"Sam asked us to interview some married couples as part of our pre-marital counseling. Would you and Mr. Patterson be willing to let us ask you some questions?"

"Of course." Susan grinned, still clutching Madeleine's hands. "Give me a call and we'll set something up."

6

"Mom, I've got some news about the wedding." It was Monday morning during his planning period. A.J. should be writing lessons but needed to get the word out about the new wedding date as soon as possible.

"What is it? Has Maddy called off the wedding again?"

A.J. slapped a hand to his forehead. "No, Mom. It's about the day of the ceremony." Madeleine had gotten cold feet and panicked the night of their engagement party, and A.J.'s mom might never let him forget about it. "We had to move up the date by a week."

"Well, you've already moved it up by a year. What's one week in the scheme of things?"

Oh, yeah. And they'd decided to get married a whole year sooner after A.J. was accepted to grad school.

"Are you still going to be able to come?" He paced around the classroom, picking up trash and abandoned pencils off the floor.

His mom sighed on the other end of the phone. "Of course, I'll be there. What could possibly be more important than my son's wedding?"

"Maybe your daughter's wedding. Do you know if Olivia is planning to get married that weekend?"

"Don't joke. You'll give me a heart attack." She let out a *hmph.* "You know I don't like that boy she's seeing right now."

A.J. couldn't possibly keep track of who Olivia was "seeing" since she hadn't actually brought a boy home or started any serious relationships. But Mom was obsessed with stalking his sisters and their friends on social media to keep up with every relationship development.

"Mark your calendars for December seventeenth. That's the Saturday before Christmas Eve." A.J. reached under a desk for a particularly large wad of paper. "The church already had a nativity play on the twenty-fourth. It was a whole thing."

"I did try to tell you how inconvenient a Christmas Eve wedding would be."

She had, many times. Although Maddy hadn't been convinced by Mom's arguments.

"Now you don't have to worry about it messing up your Christmas plans."

"Don't get passive aggressive," Mom chided. "I merely think people would've wanted to spend the holidays with family and felt bad about missing your wedding. As much as I love you and Maddy, you are *not* the reason for the season."

He had to chuckle at that. "I'm aware. Do you think I'm trying to replace Jesus by getting married at Christmas?"

The other end of the line was silent, but A.J. imagined his mom shrugging.

"Well, you don't have to worry about it now. We'll get married the week before and no one will get confused."

"Except all the people who have the wrong wedding date."

"Right. Would you tell the family about the new date? I'm calling all the groomsmen this afternoon."

"Sure thing. I'll tell Dad and the girls and call Memaw.

Although you should call her yourself soon. She'd love to hear from you."

"Yes, ma'am."

They said their goodbyes and A.J. hung up the phone.

People always talked about his mom like she was the sweetest lady in the world. And, compared to his dad, she could be very easygoing. But something about being the only boy, or being the oldest, meant his mom was always telling him what to do.

He loved his mom and wanted to make her happy, but she seemed to have a million opinions where this wedding was concerned. Only the other day she'd sent him a bunch of pictures of wedding decorations. As if he had any say in what kind of decorations they'd have at the wedding.

Dropping all the trash he'd found into the bin by the door, A.J. rounded the corner and headed over to his desk. He sent a quick text to Madeleine. Maybe he should cut himself out of the middle and let Madeleine and his mom communicate directly.

The premarital counseling book Sam had given them the day before sat on his desk. Their homework assignment for this week was to write out their backstory. It was going to take him ages to fill out. Stuff like "What are your proudest moments from childhood?" and "What kind of religious upbringing did you have?"

The question he was dreading most—and had left blank—was "How do your parents feel about your choice in a spouse?"

His gut reaction was not good. Madeleine had mostly grown up in a single-parent house. Nothing wrong with that, but they also stopped going to church after her dad left. And then her uncle died, something that left her reeling. After all of that turmoil, it was easy to see why marriage and commitment scared Maddy.

But his parents had been hurt and upset when Maddy suddenly called off their engagement. Then they'd been confused and concerned when A.J. called them to say that actually the wedding was back on and they were getting married in two months.

Part of A.J. wanted to say "So what? Who cares?" Let his family deal with their own feelings. They'd come around to Maddy and love her as much as he did someday.

But he also knew his life would be a lot easier if his mom and his future bride could get along.

Tapping the book with the tips of his fingers, A.J. looked at the happy couple on the cover. They were probably models from California. They certainly didn't look like they were in the middle of planning a wedding while simultaneously digging through emotional family history.

He flipped over the book and let the stupid couple stare lovingly into each other's eyes while smooshed against his desk for a change. Madeleine wanted the perfect wedding. A.J. knew that was impossible, but he would tear himself apart to get as close as he could to her dream.

* * *

Interview with John and Susan Patterson

AJ: How long have you two been married?

John: Since—

Susan: 1987

John: So, that was—

Susan: Thirty-five years ago. We celebrated in September with a family trip.

Madeleine: How big is your family?

John: Four kids

Susan: Two girls, two boys. And three grandkids. Want to see a picture?

Madeleine: Very cute.

A.J.: Congratulations, that's wonderful. How long did you date before you got married? And how long were you engaged?

Susan: Well …

John: Not very long. I met Susan at a friend's house the summer before.

Susan: And I was engaged to someone else at the time.

John: But I didn't let up.

Susan: No, he was very persistent. He kept writing letters even though I told him he had no chance.

John: …

Madeleine: What changed?

Susan: I realized the man I was engaged to wasn't right for me at all. And once we broke up—

John: I swooped in and asked her to marry me.

Madeleine: You didn't date at all before you got engaged'?

Susan: Nope. Our parents were shocked at first, but they came around eventually.

John: We got married a year later, and a year after that—

Susan: We had our first baby, our daughter.

Madeleine: Was that challenging? Moving so quickly into becoming parents?

John: Yes, but we wouldn't change anything.

Susan: Kids make marriage more complicated, but becoming parents united us. And now we have grandkids.

John: Which is surprisingly fun.

A.J.: How has your marriage changed over the years?

Susan: We've changed a lot about how we communicate. We're better about asking for what we need instead of assuming the other will intuitively know.

John: I stopped assuming just about anything after the first twenty years or so.

Susan: But you still know my favorite flowers.

John: Tulips.

Susan: That's right.

7

NOVEMBER

*M*adeleine was technically at work, but her mind was miles away, daydreaming about burgundy bridesmaids' dresses. She wished she could see all of the dresses in person, side-by-side with the ribbon from the decorations and the flower arrangements. There was simply no way to know if the colors she chose matched.

"Does this look right?"

Walking closer, Madeleine gazed at the painting in front of her. Bare tree branches swept across a slate blue background. The next step would be to cover the tree with leaves in all different shades of red and orange—crimson, cranberry, burgundy, copper, pumpkin, and terracotta.

"That looks wonderful." She patted the arm of the girl who'd asked her the question and continued walking around the room.

Madeleine enjoyed her part-time job of teaching group art classes for kids. Once a month on a Saturday, she'd gather with a dozen or so children in the back of the Dusty Doily antique shop in downtown Shady Springs. This month they were working on a scene of an autumn tree, perfect for November.

"Now, while we wait for this to dry a bit, let's talk about warm and cool colors."

For the next half hour, Madeleine focused her attention back on the kids. Forcing herself to forget about dresses and floral arrangements, she concentrated solely on teaching these precious kiddos how to play with different shades and how to bring highlights and shadows into their paintings.

By the end of the class, she was tired and covered in paint, but her mind was reset and washed clean.

"How's the wedding planning going?"

Until Diana brought her crashing back to reality. Madeleine stopped mid-stride.

"Fine."

Her boss stared back at her, one hand on her hip.

Maddy groaned. "I can't decide on bridesmaids' dresses and I have to order them, like, yesterday." She continued walking across the storefront, cautiously scooting around an end table and a rocking chair.

"Show me what you've got."

Maddy sidled up next to Diana behind the cash register, pulling out her cell phone. "This is the style I'm leaning toward. And this …" She opened another tab. "Is the dress I would *really* love but can't afford."

Looking at the price of the dresses, Diana whistled. "I couldn't afford that either. Are you asking the bridesmaids to pay for their own dresses?"

Madeleine winced. "I wish I could pay for them myself, but I need to save money somewhere."

"I think you're fine." Diana pointed to the screen. "As long as you don't ask them to pay for this one."

"This other dress is fine, and it comes in multiple styles. But how do I know if it will match the flowers and the ribbons I have picked out?"

Diana was the owner of the Dusty Doily and an artist herself.

Earlier in the year, Madeleine had connected with her and offered to teach kids' classes once a month as a way to bring in shoppers. Diana taught her own classes in the back room for adults.

Surely her artist friend would have some ideas of how to proceed.

"Do you have a picture of the flowers and the decorations?"

"Yes, but how do I know the colors in the pictures will be the same?"

Madeleine went ahead and pulled up photos. She had a whole folder dedicated to wedding-related pictures on her phone.

"Okay, what if you keep the red of the dresses and find a ribbon that coordinates? Forest green or black or gold would all look very nice. That way you don't have to worry about them matching."

Yes. Why had she been so focused on matching when she could coordinate?

"You're a genius!" Madeleine could kiss her friend but didn't want to scare her off. "I'll send the link to everyone now."

"Anything else you need help with?"

Madeleine sighed. "No, I think I'm okay for now."

"Good, now go clean up that back room."

✳ ✳ ✳

When Madeleine got home, she found her aunt in the kitchen.

"You got something in the mail. Looks like it might be your first RSVP." Aunt Clara was stirring something on the stove that smelled a lot like chili. She pointed to the kitchen table. "It came really quickly. They must've put it back in the mailbox right away."

A stack of bills sat next to a stack of coupon mailers, and beside them was a small envelope with her own handwriting on the outside. A thrill rushed through her. She was getting married to A.J. and someone was coming to the wedding.

With a slight tremble in her fingers, she slid open the envelope. She skimmed the reply card quickly, her wide smile morphing into a worried frown. "But this isn't right."

She showed the card to her aunt.

Clara looked up briefly from her work at the stove to see the paper Madeleine held. "What's wrong?"

"It has the wrong date." She flipped it over, but there was nothing else written on the back. "Didn't we fix the dates on the RSVP cards?"

"Yes, and we double-checked." Clara took the paper from Madeleine and examined it. "Do you think we missed this one?"

"No. I think Bill did." If the mailman had simply handed over the invitations right away like they'd asked … but it didn't help to dwell on Bill right now. "Do you think there are more wrong invitations out there?"

"There's no way to know." Clara handed the card back to Madeleine and focused her gaze on retrieving a pan from the cabinet. "Until we start getting all of the replies, we won't have any idea."

"What do I do?"

"Call them, I guess. Who is it for?"

"Someone on A.J.'s side. Lew and Tonya Young."

"Better have him give them a call and let them know."

Madeleine and A.J. already had plans to meet up that night with Sam for dinner and a counseling session. "I'll bring it with me tonight." What else could possibly go wrong with this wedding?

8

After changing into a clean sweater and freshening up her makeup, Madeleine drove to A.J.'s house. The weather had turned chilly, although she knew it would only last a few days before a warm front moved in. Arkansas rarely got truly cold weather until January, and Madeleine was determined to enjoy this crisp autumn day with a warm sweater and a pair of cute boots.

The trees of Shady Springs had embraced the fall with goldenrod, ochre, vermillion, and burnt orange leaves adorning all the trees. And a few houses here and there on her way displayed autumn wreaths and scarecrows.

A.J. didn't have any fall decorations in his yard, but she knew he had a rotting pumpkin out back and some leftover Halloween candy in his pantry. He had definitely over purchased for trick-or-treaters—possibly an intentional choice. She couldn't complain about the extra chocolate, even if she didn't need the extra calories.

"Hey, there. I hope you're hungry." A.J. called out from the kitchen when Madeleine let herself in. She had a key to his place but never needed it, since A.J. kept his door unlocked most of the time.

That's a habit we'll need to change after the wedding.

Madeleine sniffed. Notes of tomato and basil wafted from the kitchen. Setting her purse on the floor in the entryway, she walked toward the aroma. Another difference between A.J. and Madeleine—he didn't see a need for any furniture beyond what was absolutely necessary. A sofa and a recliner in the living room, table and chairs in the dining room, and a bed to sleep on at night. Madeleine wished she had a bench or console or *someplace* other than the floor to set her purse. *I've got to add a coat rack to the wedding registry.*

Furniture choices aside, A.J. had learned a thing or two in his time living alone. A meal of spaghetti with meat sauce, bread, and salad waited in the kitchen. The bread was purchased from the grocery store and the salad was from a bag, but A.J. was making the sauce from scratch, and it smelled delicious.

"I'm starving. Spending all morning with kids can really take it out of you."

"Tell me about it." A.J. scooped a healthy portion of pasta onto a plate. "Try doing it all day, every day."

"I will, starting in January." Madeleine laid two paper towels on the kitchen table as makeshift placemats, before taking one of the plates from A.J. She made a mental note to add real placemats to the registry as well. "Assuming the administration approves me as the temporary replacement while Mrs. Wade is on maternity leave."

A.J. smiled. "Are you excited to get to work with your husband in the spring?"

"Yes." Madeleine set the plate on the table and took A.J.'s hands in hers. She gently brushed the top of his knuckles with her thumbs. "I am completely, absolutely, wildly excited." She tugged on his fingers, pulling him until their bodies closed the distance between them. Their lips met in a slow kiss, full of passion and the promise of more to come.

A.J. let out a low groan before pulling back. "When will Sam be here?"

"Soon." Madeleine and A.J. were rarely alone together nowadays, and it was definitely for the best. They both wanted to wait until marriage, but their self-control was waning. "Maybe we should start having dinner in public places."

"Probably a good idea."

"Even if this will be much better than anything we could get at Mike's Diner."

They finished setting the table, and A.J. led a prayer over their food. Madeleine's heart thrilled at the fact that she was marrying such an amazing man of faith. In less than two months.

Now her heart raced with anxiety. Less than two months and so much left to do.

"Oh, we got an RSVP today."

"That's great." A.J. gave her a questioning glance. "Why do you look upset?"

Madeleine grimaced. "It's for the wrong day. I think Bill missed theirs when he gave us the invitations back."

"Who's it from?"

"Someone from your family, Lew and Tonya?" She let her sentence lilt up in a question.

A.J. nodded, chewing a bite of bread. "I don't know them well, but I know who they are. Great Uncle Lew is my grandpa's older … Never mind." He waved his hand in the air. "You probably don't care about all that."

"Would you be able to call them? I don't know how to reach them."

He nodded, tearing off another chunk of bread. "I'll ask Mom and Dad to help me out with that."

They ate for a while before A.J. spoke up. "Did you get a chance to look at the houses I sent you?"

Her brain spun for a moment, finally recalling an unanswered text from earlier that morning. Apparently, it was houses for her to look at. "I'm sorry, babe." She bit her lip. "I was at work and then forgot to take a look."

She could tell he was disappointed from the way his eyes crinkled, but A.J. smiled and pulled out his phone. "That's okay. Here."

Swiping through the photos of a midcentury ranch-style home, Madeleine tried to show appreciation. "Not bad. And it's reasonably priced too." The house wasn't dazzling, but it looked like it had been taken care of and wouldn't need a lot of work.

"I'm setting up appointments for the week of Thanksgiving when we're in Little Rock with my family. But we could take a trip anytime to see something if our realtor finds a great house for us."

Anytime? She couldn't simply pull up and leave for a three-hour drive to Central Arkansas while she was trying to plan their wedding.

Madeleine nodded. "I'll take a look at the other houses tonight, I promise."

A.J. chewed thoughtfully before changing the subject. "What did you think about the homework for this week?"

Too bad she was unprepared for this conversation as well.

"Hmm." Madeleine chewed a bite of salad. She dabbed her lips with her napkin then took a sip of water. "It was interesting. What did *you* think?"

The grimace on his face showed that, clearly, A.J. could see right through her. She hadn't done the homework.

He pursed his lips before answering. "I appreciated the challenge of thinking about the expectations I'm bringing into our marriage. As much as I love my parents, I don't want to have a relationship that mirrors theirs. I want ours to be different." A.J. stabbed a bite of pasta with his fork. "I assume you'd say the same."

"Of course."

"You didn't read the chapter, did you?" He stuck the bite of spaghetti in his mouth, a little too forcefully.

"I mean …" She pushed a crouton around her salad. "I didn't *not* read it. I definitely skimmed it."

"Maddy." A.J. groaned, and this time it was all annoyance and none of the desire from earlier. "This is really important. You can't skim through premarital counseling."

"I *know* it's really important. That's why I'm here and not going over the catering menu right now."

A.J.'s eyebrows shot up.

"And to spend time with you, of course," Madeleine added. Her heart rate picked up. She was slowly drowning in wedding details. And now A.J. was adding to her plate with guilt over not focusing enough on houses and premarital counseling.

His eyes closed, A.J. slowly blew out a breath. Madeleine imagined him counting to ten in his head. If this wasn't the most patient man in the world, she'd eat her hat. Or her autumn scarf, since she didn't have a hat. Sometimes she wished he would just yell at her and get all of his frustration out of his system.

"I feel like you aren't taking this seriously."

"Which part? Because I've been working my tail off to get our wedding ceremony off the ground."

A.J. pulled his lips tight.

"And I don't see you bending over backward to help out."

"I helped with the registry." He set his fork down.

The registry? The easiest part of the whole planning process? She rolled her eyes.

"What do you want me to do? I'm trying to work full-time, find a house for us to live in, and plan the honeymoon." He sat back in his seat, folding his arms. "But if you want me to pick flower arrangements and decorations, I'll do it."

She physically recoiled at the thought of A.J. selecting

decorations for their wedding. That sounded like an actual nightmare. "No."

"Then what do you want?"

"I want …" What did she want?

The doorbell rang.

Madeleine and A.J. stared at each other for a beat. What should they do?

A.J. stood first, pushing his chair back. Madeleine stayed in the kitchen, using the chore of dishes as an excuse to take a moment to think. A.J.'s plate was empty, and she wasn't hungry anymore.

"Hi, Sam. Come on in." A.J.'s voice sounded upbeat, as if they hadn't just paused mid-argument to answer the door.

Madeleine pasted a smile on her face before poking her head around the kitchen wall. "I'm just cleaning up our dishes. I'll be right there."

Sam shot back a cautious smile and wave. Her false enthusiasm must not be convincing.

"Would you like something to drink?"

"No, thanks."

Madeleine rinsed each plate, fork, and knife, sliding them into the dishwasher when she was finished. She took a steadying breath. One way or another, she was going to get through this counseling session. Might as well get it over with.

Madeleine grabbed her workbook from her purse and settled into the couch beside A.J. Sam sat opposite them in the recliner.

"Let's talk about the expectations you're bringing into your marriage." Sam opened his book, turning to the third chapter. "This usually comes from the way your family of origin operates, but we can have expectations based on society and media."

A.J. nodded, pulling out his own copy of their workbook.

"Did you have a chance to compare notes? Did anything stick out to you as a difference?"

"Um, no." Madeleine lowered her gaze, but from the corner of her eye, she could see A.J. looking at her. "We didn't get a chance to compare."

"That's okay. We can go over it now."

Madeleine flipped to the page Sam and A.J. were on. From glancing at A.J., she could tell his pages were full of scribbled answers to every question.

She looked down at her own workbook. Her field of vision blurred, but she blinked to clear her eyes. Of course, A.J. was mad at her. She'd done a terrible job of preparing for their counseling sessions so far.

"I'm sorry, I—" She swallowed, pushing down the lump in her throat. "I didn't actually do the lesson yet."

"Thank you for your honesty." Sam's voice was gentle. "Let's talk through it, and I can guide you with the questions."

A.J.'s fingers wrapped around hers. He squeezed hard once before stroking the back of her hand with his thumb.

Sam didn't pull any punches with his first question. "How did your parents model conflict and resolution? What would you like to carry forward or leave behind from their example?"

A.J. answered first. "My parents didn't argue too much growing up. But I saw my dad get his way a lot. There were times it seemed like family issues simply got ignored." He squeezed Madeleine's hand once before letting go. "I'd like to have more transparency in our marriage."

"That's very insightful. Thanks, A.J." Sam turned to Madeleine, an expectant expression on his face.

"Right." Madeleine sighed. "When I was young, my parents fought a lot. It got worse and worse until one day my dad left." She dug her fingers into the knitted fabric of her sweater. "I went through a really difficult time during my teen years and—" She grimaced, glancing to Sam and A.J. "You both know all of this."

"That's okay," Sam said. "You get a turn to answer the question too."

Madeleine twisted the hem of her sweater around her thumb. "Sometimes when A.J. and I fight, I want to run away and hide. I start to panic. I know that our relationship is different—I know you aren't my dad." She looked up from her sweater to A.J.'s gaze. "So I guess I'm saying I want our relationship to feel safe."

"I agree." A.J. smiled softly, leaning toward her. "I want to be someone you aren't afraid to disagree with."

"I'm working on it." Madeleine nudged A.J.'s shoulder with hers. "I just need help getting there."

As Sam led them through question by question, her angst slowly disappeared. Finding she was on the same page as A.J. lifted the tension from her chest. By the end of the night, Madeleine could breathe easily again. "I promise to do my homework next week."

"I believe you." Sam gripped her shoulder, giving her a reassuring smile, before heading out the door.

Madeleine sighed and turned to A.J. with a wince on her face. "I'm sorry again. I know our premarital counseling is important."

A.J. pulled her into a hug, wrapping his arms around her and rocking back and forth. He kissed her on the top of the head. "Thank you. I'm sorry if I was too hard on you. I'm learning right along with you."

Breathing deeply, Madeleine relished the clean smell of his shirt. Squeezing her eyes shut, she let herself imagine a quiet night at home with her husband. The patterns and rituals of married life. She couldn't wait to wake up next to him every morning. But she would have to—wait, that is.

Less than two months.

But what if it wasn't enough time to become the wife she wanted to be? What if she couldn't give A.J. the marriage he deserved?

9

A.J. hadn't gone home to Little Rock since summer break, and it felt good to be heading south for Thanksgiving. His parents would be hosting aunts and uncles and cousins, but they promised to save a bed and a sofa for him and Madeleine. He tried not to dwell on the fact that they wouldn't have to sleep apart in only a month.

Although they *did* need to think about sharing a house. Other than celebrating the holiday with family, the primary reason for coming early to Little Rock was house hunting in nearby Sayers.

He wanted something small and close to Halloway School of Theology, the place he'd be spending the next three years. Madeleine hadn't been forthcoming with what she wanted in a home, but he assumed that was because she'd been preoccupied with wedding planning. Surely once she was faced with the reality of their move, she'd have a little more input into the big decisions.

Even though he wasn't starting classes until May, A.J. wanted to explore the housing market in Sayers. He needed to be familiar with the neighborhoods and prepared to buy a home sooner rather than later. Before they knew it, winter break would be over, the spring semester would be upon them, and they'd be left without any good options.

"Here we are." Flicking on the turn indicator, he slowed to a stop before making a right into his parents' neighborhood. A.J. nudged Madeleine with his elbow, jolting her awake.

"Are we here already?"

"You've been out for over an hour." He chuckled at her sleepy frown.

"I'm sorry." She wiped a hand over her face, then smoothed her hair into a ponytail.

"No problem. It gave me a chance to catch up on sports podcasts."

"Do I look okay?" She was already pulling down the windshield visor and checking her face in the mirror.

He gave a quick glance before answering, "You look wonderful."

The rest of his extended family wouldn't be visiting until Thursday, so they were greeted by a relatively quiet house. Even his sisters were gone, both of them out shopping for groceries, according to the family group text.

"Hellooo!" His mom raced to the door to hug them both. "How was your drive?" She took bags from Madeleine and pulled them inside.

Fresh vacuum lines covered the plush carpet, mirrors sparkled, and each pillow was perfectly arranged on the sofa.

"The place looks great, Mom."

"Oh, I'm still hoping to dust the baseboards and hang a few more pictures before your grandparents get here." She smiled sheepishly. "But thank you. Are you hungry? Thirsty?"

After unloading the car and dropping off suitcases, A.J. and Madeleine joined his mom at the kitchen counter. A.J. grabbed a soda for himself and water for Madeleine.

"What's your schedule for the next couple days? Were you able to set up any appointments to look at houses?"

"Yes. This afternoon and all day tomorrow. I'm hoping to make an offer on something while we're here."

He looked to Madeleine for confirmation, but she was checking something on her phone.

"Your aunts and uncles will get here Wednesday night." His mom wiped the perfectly clean counters with a kitchen rag. "And I volunteered you to lead a prayer at our devotional that evening. I hope you don't mind."

"Of course not."

"Maddy, dear. Are you still planning to help make the mac and cheese?"

Madeleine glanced up from her phone. "I'm sorry, I was just —what was it you said?"

"The macaroni and cheese?"

"Yes." She set the phone in her lap. "We brought in the boxes, and I'll pick up some butter and milk before Thursday."

Boxes? He shared a look with his mom. Who made macaroni and cheese from a box on Thanksgiving?

"Thank you. That sounds wonderful." Mom smiled at Madeleine before turning back to the fridge. "I'm going to get dinner prepped. Are either of you hungry? Did you eat lunch?"

"We grabbed food on the way. And we've got to meet our realtor soon."

"Already?" Madeleine gulped some water, then stood up. "Let me grab my purse."

While she was out of the room, A.J. whispered to his mom. "I'm happy you're trying to make an effort with Madeleine, but don't feel like you have to let her cook for Thanksgiving."

His mom raised her eyebrows. "Let her? I need all the help I can get."

"Okay." He tapped the kitchen counter and stood up. "Well, thanks. It means a lot."

If his mom really was coming around to Madeleine, his life was about to get a whole lot easier.

* * *

"Okay, this last house was listed only a few days ago." Lisa, the realtor, grinned as she pulled up a sheet of information about the property. "It's really cute inside, has a lot of potential, and is priced right."

A.J. raised his eyebrows and bit his lip to keep himself from saying something mean about the tiny shack they stood in front of. He knew Madeleine had been less than impressed with the two houses they'd already seen. The first reeked of cigarette smoke, and the second had clearly been home to many pets over the years.

This one had a flowerbed that had seen better days and a porch railing that needed repairing, but there was a garage, so that was nice.

"I like that archway." Madeleine pointed out when they walked inside.

"Thanks."

Shocked, A.J., Madeleine, and Lisa turned to see an older man walking through the archway in question.

"Hi, I'm Vince."

"Nice to meet you, Vince." A.J. stuck out his hand. "I'm A.J. and this is my fiancé, Madeleine."

Vince led them on a tour of the kitchen. Surprisingly, it had a few updated appliances, even if they were cramped together.

The home boasted original wood paneling in both bedrooms and the living room. And one of the bathrooms was, inexplicably, carpeted.

"The guest bathroom is really comfortable. It has a double sink and a full-sized tub." Vince waved his hand out as if he were showcasing a new car on a game show.

Madeleine stepped in first nodding appreciatively. "Very nice." She pulled back the curtain to look at the tub, and immediately stepped back, squeezing A.J.'s arm in a death grip.

A large, black roach scurried out of the drain. A.J. shuddered as it raced across the edge of the tub and down to the floor, crawling through a hole in the baseboard.

Lisa and Vince seemed not to notice, talking cheerfully through the whole incident.

A.J. grabbed Madeleine's hand and tugged her toward the front room. "Thank you so much, Vince. It was great meeting you."

Madeleine grimaced and gave a falsely cheery wave. "Yes, thank you."

Once they were out of earshot and close to the car, A.J. took Madeleine by the shoulders. "I will never make you live there. Even if we have to live with my parents for the next three years, I will make sure we live in a clean house."

Madeleine nodded, biting her lip.

"I can't promise we'll never have any flies or spiders. But I'll do my best not to buy a home with an active roach problem."

As soon as they were back in the car, Madeleine's shoulders began to shake. Was she crying? He was an awful future husband for dragging her through all of these run-down houses. She must be terrified to start a life together, having seen a preview of what it might look like.

"Maddy? Are you okay?"

A squeak came from her lips. He rested a hand on her arm.

She turned, and a breath rushed out of him. Laughter took over her whole face and body. She giggled uncontrollably. "I can't—" She gasped. "I mean, when the—" She skittered her fingers over an imaginary tub. "And then it—" She collapsed into her hands. "Oh, my."

A.J. joined in the hilarity. Maybe she was losing her mind, but at least he hadn't made Madeleine cry.

Lisa tapped on the window. "Hey." She gave Madeleine a bemused smile, then turned her gaze to A.J. "I know today was a bit disappointing. I've got some more houses lined up for tomorrow, and we'll be sure to take a look at anything that goes on the market tonight. Don't worry. This is a fast-moving market, and we have new properties available every day."

"Thanks, Lisa. See you tomorrow." A.J. turned the key in his pickup. "Let's go home." He patted Madeleine's knee.

Cockroaches. He clenched his shoulders and grimaced.

Sure hope Lisa has something better in store for tomorrow. Otherwise, we've completely wasted two of our already overbudgeted days.

10

"Look what came in the mail today!"

Madeleine glanced up from the puzzle she was working on with A.J. and his dad, Arthur. She never knew exactly what to call him. Her parents, who'd known him in college, called him Artie. Ginger and the rest of the family called him Arthur. She mostly called him Mr. Young, and he hadn't corrected her so far. She'd certainly never call him "Dad" like A.J. and his sisters.

Felicity, A.J.'s youngest sister, stood across the room with a brown package in her hands. "Look, Maddy. The return address is from the dress company."

Standing as quickly as possible—without knocking over the puzzle table—Madeleine rushed to Felicity's side. "Let's go open it in your room."

"Mom! We're trying on the bridesmaid dress," Felicity yelled down the hall before racing up the stairs to her room, Madeleine hot on her heels.

Carefully, Felicity cut through the tape with a pair of scissors from her desk drawer. A gorgeous burgundy fabric peeked through the opening.

Madeleine held her breath.

Opening the flaps, Felicity pulled out the dress and held it up.

Hmm.

Something didn't look quite like the pictures.

"Let me try it on." Felicity pulled on the dress and twisted side-to-side in front of the full-length mirror in the corner.

A knock sounded on the door before Ginger turned the knob and walked in. "Oh my."

On either side of Felicity's dress, two giant holes had been cut out. It was obviously intentional on the part of the designer, but not what Madeleine wanted.

"I didn't realize."

"This won't do." Ginger *tsked* with her hands on her hips.

"This is the style now, Mom." Felicity certainly had the figure to pull off the cut-out style, but Madeleine wasn't hoping to push the envelope with her bridesmaids' dresses.

"I'm so sorry. I had no idea from the website."

"Could we wear a turtleneck underneath maybe?" Ginger gently tugged at the sides of the opening, but nothing was fixing this problem.

"I'm afraid it would look tacky."

"Yeah, Mom. It would look super tacky."

Ginger pursed her lips, clearly thinking that nothing could look tackier than the current situation.

"We've got to return the dresses." Madeleine sank to the fuzzy chair by Felicity's desk. She shook her head. "But I have no idea what to do now. That was the only dress I found that was the right color and reasonably priced."

Her phone buzzed. It was a text from Staci, one of the other bridesmaids.

> I look cute but this dress might be a little cold
> for December …

Below the message was a picture of Staci, reflected in a mirror and making a goofy face.

Madeleine dropped her cell back in her lap and rubbed her temples with her fingers.

Another knock at the door and A.J. was in the room.

"Hey, Maddy, we need to—" He froze, looking at Felicity with wide eyes. "What in the world are you wearing?"

Felicity turned, with a teasing smile on her face, holding the hem of the skirt in a curtsy. "My bridesmaid dress for your wedding. What do you think?"

His mouth flapped open like a fish gasping for air. A.J. turned to Madeleine. No words came at first, but his expression said it all.

"We're returning the dresses." Madeleine was not in the mood to tease or participate in any more family dramatics.

A.J. clamped his mouth shut again. "We need to look at the listings Lisa just sent. Whenever you get a minute." He practically sprinted out of the room.

As Felicity changed back into her jeans and sweatshirt, Madeleine pulled up the link for the dresses again. "See? There was no way to know that there was a cutout."

The picture on the website showed the dress from different vantage points, but never at an angle that showed the sides properly. And the model was bent or obscured in every picture.

Ginger patted her shoulder. "We didn't spot it when we ordered either."

"What am I going to do now?"

"We could always go shopping for something here in Little Rock." Felicity sat on the bed and gave Madeleine a sympathetic pout.

"And we can scour the internet until we find something suitable." Ginger folded the dress—which really was the absolute perfect color—and stuffed it back into the box.

Time was slipping away. Only one month until the wedding

and now they had no bridesmaids' dresses. She closed her eyes and silently prayed.

Lord, I really wanted this wedding to be perfect. Why is everything falling apart?

* * *

Later that evening, Madeleine sat beside A.J. on the living room sofa, staring at his laptop.

"What do you think about this one?" He clicked on a tab for a real estate listing. If nothing else, the photography was good. It was a house built in the early 2000s, one story, three bedrooms, two bathrooms, and a two-car garage. It looked like someone had taken care of the property.

"It's nice." Madeleine shifted in her seat, snuggling into A.J.'s side.

"But …?" A.J. trailed off.

"It's fine." Madeleine couldn't technically find anything wrong with the house. But its white walls, beige carpet, and flowerbeds of plain boxwood held zero interest. "It's just kind of boring."

"Okay." A.J. clicked through the pictures again. "Boring could be good, though, right?"

"Sure." Madeleine supposed he was right. A boring house meant fewer problems to deal with. And they'd be able to move in with no issues.

"What else do we have?" Madeleine waited as A.J. clicked on the next open internet tab.

"How about this one?" A.J. pulled up another listing, this time for a red brick home built in the eighties.

"Okay, not bad." It was certainly interesting, but not necessarily in a good way. The windows were too small, the ceilings were too low, and the carpet looked dingy.

"It might need some fixing up, but at least it's less expensive."

Madeleine sighed as A.J. closed his laptop. "Is being an adult always this hard?"

"No." A.J. wrapped his arm around her shoulders. "Sometimes it's fun."

"Looking for a house is supposed to be fun."

"Sure, it's fun when you're simply looking. But actually trying to buy a house can be stressful." He leaned his head against hers. "We have a while until May. If we don't see something we like on this trip, we still have time. Lisa said people list new houses on the market every day."

"You're right." Madeleine nudged A.J. with her shoulder. "At least I know I'll have a great roommate."

But as Madeleine squeezed her eyes tight and whispered a silent prayer of blessing on their house hunting, an unwelcome thought invaded her mind. What if finding a perfect home was every bit as difficult as planning the perfect wedding?

She didn't want a mansion. No granite countertops, marble columns, or stained-glass windows. She only wanted a quiet, peaceful place to start her married life with A.J.

But what if God was holding something back?

What if He was trying to tell her *not yet*—or worse—*not this.*

Tendrils of fear pushed through her chest. Tomorrow they'd tour more houses and try to imagine a life inside of them. But what if none of them felt right? What would that mean?

If tomorrow didn't reveal some decent places, she didn't know what she'd do.

11

The next morning was spent touring the two houses they'd seen online the night before. Seeing them in person didn't raise Madeleine's first impressions, but she tried not to show her disappointment.

"I could see us in this house." A.J. walked around the living room of the newer home, the white and beige house. "What do you think?"

"It's much nicer than the eighties house, that's for sure." Madeleine frowned as she stared at the frilly glass light covers on the brass and white ceiling fan above her. The whole house had fake brass hardware. But that could be fixed easily enough.

"I have one more house to show you today. This one isn't on the market yet, but my client wants to list it in the spring." Lisa shared the address with them before getting into her car.

Slightly curious, but not overly hopeful, Madeleine buckled into the passenger seat of A.J.'s truck.

They traveled down the main highway in town until they came to an older neighborhood close to campus. A.J. drove down a smaller road until Lisa's car stopped. He parked his truck on the side of the street behind her.

Madeleine stepped out of the car and onto the front lawn of a 1930s Tudor-style cottage with yellow brick and an arched entryway. The concrete walkway and flowerbeds had seen better days, but that could be fixed. A maple tree boasted bright scarlet leaves, the prettiest on the whole block.

Even from the outside, the home oozed charm. Madeleine allowed herself a small smile, but steeled herself for disappointment once they entered.

Lisa knocked three times quickly on the door, and an older woman in jeans and a green sweater greeted them. "I'll stay out of your hair while you look around."

"Thank you so much for letting us take a look at your home." Madeleine smiled at her as they walked inside.

The living room was packed with overstuffed chairs and sofas. Almost the opposite of A.J.'s barren bachelor pad. A large floral rug sat in the middle of the floor, twin lamps rested on two end tables, and a large tasseled floor lamp hung over an armchair close to the fireplace. Doilies, books, and tchotchkes were sprinkled throughout.

The smell was a little musty, and dust floated in the air like glitter, but none of that mattered to Madeleine. She stepped on light feet through the living room and into the kitchen. Twin leaded glass windows framed the kitchen sink. She could practically see singing woodland creatures peeking through. This was the sort of kitchen where birds flew in and crimped your pie crust for you while whistling a cheery tune.

The rooms were a little cramped, and the bathroom had pink tile and a matching pink tub, something Madeleine couldn't decide if she loved or disliked. The floors creaked, and the back door let in a draft.

Back outside, Madeleine tugged A.J.'s elbow. "I want to live in this house."

A.J. winced. "Are you sure? I can already tell it's going to need a lot of work. And we're not going to be able to afford to hire a contractor. We'll have to do the work ourselves."

That thought made her pause but only a moment. She thought of singing woodland creatures. "Yes, I'm sure."

"It is close to campus …" A.J. kicked a dirt clod. "Are you sure you want this house?"

"I know it's not perfect, but there's something about this place that's really special."

"Okay." He shrugged nonchalantly, but smiled at her. "I'll talk to Lisa."

Lisa and the homeowner stood in the doorway chatting.

"We really love your home." Madeleine stepped onto the porch. "How long have you lived here?"

"Since about 1995. We moved here after my husband retired and the kids moved out. After he died, it was too much to keep up by myself, so I'm moving to a retirement community."

"Did either of you work on campus?" A.J. asked.

"Yes, he was a professor at Halloway."

Madeleine grinned and pointed at A.J. "He just got accepted to the theology school. That's why we're moving to Sayers."

The woman's smile was like a ray of sunshine. "That's wonderful. I'd love to see a young couple in this house."

They chatted a bit more and said goodbye to Lisa and the woman.

"I'll let you know what I hear. Have a Happy Thanksgiving!" Lisa waved before getting in her car and driving away.

A.J. opened the passenger door of his truck for Madeleine. "Not much longer."

Normally, that reminder would twist her gut with anxiety. But today, Madeleine only felt happy. "Not much longer."

* * *

"Do you have a minute to talk?" A.J. found his dad in a rare moment of repose, resting on the couch in the living room. He and Madeleine had made a lot of progress on the puzzle that morning, nearly all of the autumn farmhouse scene completed on the coffee table.

He hated to ruin a nice moment, but he needed to have a conversation with his dad. One he'd been putting off for far too long.

Currently, Madeleine and Mom were looking through Mom's address book to find Great-Uncle Lew's phone number so they could tell him about the new date for the wedding.

"Sure, what's going on?"

"It's about the wedding."

Dad tensed, his mustache twitched, but he continued to stare at the puzzle, a red piece in his hand. "What about it?"

"I had hoped you and Mom would help pay a little for the rehearsal dinner and ceremony."

For many years, Mom and Dad had reminded A.J. and his sisters that they planned to contribute financially to their weddings. There was a time when A.J. wasn't sure if he'd ever get to tap into those savings. He didn't mind a modest ceremony, but Madeleine and her parents were stressed to the breaking point with expenses. Besides all that, he needed to know if Dad would actually follow through on his promise.

"We will." Dad found the spot for the red piece, on a large hole in the middle where the image of a barn would be.

"The wedding is in less than a month, and Madeleine's family could use the help. Maddy really wants to get something nailed down for the rehearsal dinner soon."

Dad stirred the pieces around on the table, frowning. "How much are you thinking?"

"Not much, enough for fifty people or so." That was counting the bridal party and close family. "There's a restaurant across the street from the church building that caters events. We've had their sandwiches at school before."

"I'll talk to your mom. She and Madeleine can work something out, I'm sure."

It was a yes. Sort of.

A.J. leaned back on the sofa, but he couldn't shake the unease growing in his gut.

"Can I ask you something?" A.J. said quietly. "Do you even want to be part of this?"

Dad froze.

"I just … I guess I wanted a little excitement from you. A crumb of enthusiasm, maybe. You seem like you don't even care that I'm getting married."

His dad smiled as he found a home for another puzzle piece, but his demeanor changed as he focused back on A.J. "Of course I care. This wedding is happening a lot faster than we were prepared for."

A.J.'s heart sank. His expression must have given him away —his dad scowled back at him.

"I've got to save up for your sisters. With tuition expenses, and now Olivia is seeing someone … before I know it, she'll be getting married too." He let the brown puzzle piece drop from his hand.

A.J. took a moment to truly look at his father.

He'd always been told he was the spitting image of his dad. Same red hair, same facial features. Except A.J. was usually happy and Dad was usually tense, which meant their expressions were always different enough to keep them from being mistaken for each other. Plus, Dad's big bushy mustache was a choice A.J. would never make for himself.

Today, though, Dad's face was drawn. The corners of his eyes turned down and the skin between his eyebrows creased. He almost looked … sad.

"Dad, are you okay? You seem down."

"I'm fine." He hastily picked the brown puzzle piece back up and snapped it into its place on the trunk of the tree in the picture.

"All of your kids are growing up and moving out. I'm getting married and the girls aren't far behind."

Dad grunted, sifting through the small pile of loose puzzle pieces. A.J.'s shoulders softened as he watched his father. Sending his kids out into the world had been harder on him than A.J. realized.

"But aren't you happy I found a good wife? And I finally found a career path that fits me. I'm doing great. You did a good job raising all of us."

"I'm happy you found Madeleine. Your mom and I like her a lot." Dad raised his gaze to meet A.J.'s. "I wish you weren't rushing into this wedding. And I wish you'd chosen a more profitable career. Being a preacher is tough work and doesn't pay much."

A.J. stiffened. "I didn't choose preaching for the money. I chose it because I believe it's where God called me to be."

"No one does." Dad snorted a laugh. "But you've never had to pay bills for a growing family. You don't yet understand the implications of your choice."

What could he say? A.J. was firm in his decision to become a minister. He just had to wait for Dad's heart to soften.

Silence stretched between them, broken only by the soft scratch of puzzle pieces on the coffee table.

Finally, Dad took his eyes off the puzzle, turning to face A.J. "If I'm being honest …" He paused, stroking his mustache. "I miss you and your sisters more than I thought I would."

"Aw, Dad." A.J. reached over and jostled Dad's leg. "I didn't know you were such a softie."

"If I pay for an expensive dinner and ceremony, what kind of expectation does that set up for the rest of the marriage? I can't finance your new life together. You have to take care of yourselves from now on."

Ah, back to the finances. Dad could only take about thirty seconds to talk about feelings before he was on to more practical topics.

"Dad, you didn't raise me to be irresponsible. I own a home. I have *equity* for crying out loud." A.J. glanced over at the puzzle. A bright orange piece caught his eye.

"We'll help out. Just like we promised." Dad's lips twitched in what could possibly be a smile. "What are you thinking about for a honeymoon? I overheard you telling Mom you're planning that part of the wedding."

"I was hoping we could visit someplace warm. Maybe Florida or a cruise." He imagined Madeleine would be ready to get away from it all after the wedding was over. A memory surfaced. "Doesn't Mom have a friend from church who works as a travel agent?"

"Hmm." Dad cleared his throat. "Tell you what. You want someplace warm? I have a friend with some rental properties in Texas and Louisiana. I'll see if I can get a good deal and let you know."

Wow. A.J. wasn't expecting that. "That would be a huge help, Dad. Thanks."

He popped the orange piece into the correct spot on the first try.

A bubble of laughter welled up in his chest. He'd had a breakthrough today. He'd faced the difficult conversation and come out on the other side unscathed. Maybe all those counseling sessions with Sam and Madeleine were starting to pay off. He and his dad weren't on the same page yet. But they were at least reading from the same chapter.

A.J. let out a slow exhale, stretching his legs and studying the puzzle again. Nearly finished. But from where he sat, a gap still yawned in the middle—just big enough to make the picture unfinished.

Tomorrow was Thanksgiving and the house would fill with food, family, and a whole lot of opinions. The noise, the laughter, the chatter. And then it was back to regular life and the looming wedding.

Maybe—if they were lucky—the pieces would finally start to fall into place.

Or maybe, they'd realize something was still missing.

12

The Young family kitchen was a scene of absolute chaos. Timers beeped, apron-clad aunts and cousins bustled around countertops, and steam escaped from pots.

A.J. was a decent cook. He might even be helpful on a normal day. But not today. Even the question "How can I help?" would be met with menacing glares on Thanksgiving Day. So he grabbed forks and knives and napkins to set the table and hightailed it out of there.

When the food was finally ready, his uncles had fallen asleep in front of the television, and younger cousins were racing around outside. Rounding up the family took another ten minutes, but at long last, they all gathered together. Each person grabbed a hand, the circle stretching from the dining room to the living room.

While his dad led a prayer, A.J. squeezed Madeleine's hand. He peeked one eye open at her. She was handling the noisy family holiday like a champ. She'd met some family members here and there, but this was her first time seeing everyone together. And he'd already had multiple people tell him how happy they were about the wedding. Everyone loved her.

They all said "Amen" and grabbed plates to load up with turkey and all the fixings. A.J. made sure to take a small portion of Madeleine's mac and cheese. He was willing to try anything, even if it wasn't made the way he was used to.

Madeleine took a seat by Dad, and A.J. joined her. Most of his cousins were too old for the kids' table now, so they'd started mixing generations. Some were at the long dining room table, some at the kitchen table, and some at a card table.

"Mm." A.J. chewed a bite of turkey. As good as that bird could possibly taste. "Great job on the turkey, Mom."

His mom smiled from the other end of the table.

He sampled the rest of the plate. Green beans with bacon from his Aunt Paula, sweet potato casserole made by his grandma, rolls that one of his cousins brought. He made sure to loudly compliment each dish.

Last, he dug his fork into Madeleine's macaroni and cheese. Already, it looked a little bland. And it was probably cold from sitting on his plate so long.

He took a bite, swallowing quickly.

"What do you think?" Madeleine stared at him, her eyes round and expectant.

"It's fine."

She nodded, tight-lipped, and went back to eating from her plate.

He should probably explain his perspective. "It's just not how my mom always makes it."

As he circled back around his plate for another bite of *almost* every dish, he caught his mom staring at him from across the room. She gave him a pointed glance, her eyebrows raised nearly to her hairline.

What?

He shrugged it off and ate another forkful of turkey.

"I love the macaroni and cheese." Dad spoke up from his seat.

Madeleine gave him a small smile before returning her gaze to her food.

After he'd gone back for seconds and eaten as much as he comfortably could, A.J. helped clear the table. He'd give his stomach time to settle before he nabbed a slice of Grandma's pumpkin pie.

Unlike the preparation of the food, the cleaning up of the dishes was a quieter affair. The kitchen still bore the marks of the chaos that morning. The counters were splattered and pans lay every which way on top of the stove, as if a bomb had gone off.

But no one was mad at him when he offered to help out. And no one kicked him out of the kitchen while he washed dishes. His aunts and grandma visited at their tables, while his cousins wrangled children or went back for more helpings of food. Only A.J. and his mom stood at the sink.

"Great meal, Mom."

"I had lots of help." She took a dish from his hands and dried it with a towel. She stacked it on the counter and smiled at him. "But thank you."

A.J. scrubbed a particularly difficult pan. Brown stuck-on food ringed the edges.

"I thought Madeleine's macaroni and cheese was tasty."

He grunted in assent while he plunged his gloved hands into the warm, soapy water. What did she want him to say? It was fine, but certainly nothing special.

"Did I ever tell you about the first time I met your Granny and Grandpa Young?"

"Sure, Granny made some comment about how tall you are."

Mom chuckled. "Yes, but have I told you about the cookies she made?"

"No." A.J. racked his brain, but he couldn't remember that part of the story.

"They were the strangest-tasting cookies I've ever eaten. We found out later she'd switched the salt and sugar in the recipe. I think she burned them too." She laughed, shaking her head.

"But she's such a great cook."

His mom patted his shoulder before reaching for another dish to dry. "She is. But everyone makes mistakes sometimes." She took the dish to the cabinet. "My point is, the cookies were terrible. And your father has never been one to hold back his true opinions."

A.J. rolled his eyes, recalling all the times he'd been on the receiving end of Dad's criticism. "Don't I know it."

"Well, Gramps came to her defense. He took a big bite of a cookie, chewed it up, and said, 'Best cookie I've ever eaten.'"

His Gramps had been a kind man. A.J. missed his presence, especially during the holidays.

"Your father and I both learned a lesson that day. Some silly cookies were way less important to Gramps than loving and supporting his wife." Mom set the dish towel on the counter. "Madeleine and I are different people. There are a lot of things we won't do the same way."

"I know that." A.J. kept his eyes trained on the dishwater, pretending to be preoccupied with the job of cleaning a serving fork. Truthfully, he was embarrassed to be getting a lecture from his mom on relationships. He should know better.

"Perhaps you should let Madeleine know that you know. She'd appreciate an apology, I'm sure." She picked up the damp towel from the counter and flicked her wrist, slapping him in the leg with it. "And if you care so much about how the macaroni and cheese is made, volunteer to make it yourself next time."

Point taken.

Now how could he apologize to Madeleine without making her even more upset?

13

"I'm sorry."

Madeleine looked up from her laptop, blinking until her vision focused on A.J. He stood with his shoulder pressed against the doorframe of his childhood bedroom.

The room told stories of a younger A.J. Photos and posters and trophies surrounded her. A.J.'s kindness in sleeping on the couch meant she'd spent each night snuggled in his old t-shirt quilt. This week had allowed her to see another side of him, the boy he once was.

"Pardon?" she asked, her fingers still hovering over the keyboard.

"I'm sorry." He walked into the room, leaving the door open. "I shouldn't have said what I did about the mac and cheese. It was rude."

Madeleine tilted her head. "You're apologizing about *that*?"

The mattress sagged under his weight as A.J. sat beside her. "Yes. I shouldn't have said what I did. I know it wasn't a huge thing, but I hurt your feelings, and I don't like doing that."

Madeleine glanced down at the quilt in her lap. "It's not a crime to like your mom's cooking better." She didn't cook a lot, and his mom probably made him lots of delicious meals growing up.

"No." A.J. took her hand in his. "But it is a crime to be such a clueless idiot."

She couldn't help but laugh.

"I love you a whole lot more than any food." A.J. went on, a twinkle in his eye. "Even mac and cheese. And I really love mac and cheese."

"Thanks. I love you more than mac and cheese too." She leaned into his shoulder, letting his apology sink in.

"And my mom wants me to acknowledge that you might cook some foods differently than I had growing up, and that's okay."

Madeleine straightened, giving him a sidelong glance. "She did?"

His ears reddened. "Yes, in classic Mom fashion she made me see the error of my ways by holding a mirror in my face."

"Did she tell you to come apologize?"

"I was going to apologize," A.J. muttered.

"Eventually." Madeleine bumped his arm with her shoulder.

"Eventually." A.J. laughed.

A smile tugged at her lips. "But she got you to say you're sorry. Which means maybe she doesn't hate me."

"No, she definitely doesn't. Mom just takes a long time to warm up." He grinned. "Like Aunt Paula's slow cooker of green beans."

This time Madeleine let the grin take over her whole face. Maybe she and Ginger wouldn't become best friends overnight, but they weren't stuck on opposite sides anymore.

"I can work with that."

* * *

"Bye. We'll text when we make it back to Shady Springs." Madeleine gave Ginger and Arthur—he'd asked her to call him Arthur instead of Mr. Young—a hug each.

"Did you take some cans of soda? And cookies? Do you need any cash?" Ginger wrung her hands, peering through the windows of A.J.'s truck to make sure they were well-stocked.

"We have everything we need, Mom. Thank you." A.J. squeezed his mom in a hug. Madeleine smiled.

"Bye, Dad." A.J. slapped his dad on the back.

"Drive safe."

Madeleine and A.J. waved to Ginger and Arthur until they were too far away to see. Sighing, Madeleine leaned back in her seat. "That was a good visit. I like your family."

"They like you too." A.J. glanced briefly in her direction.

"And aside from the bridesmaids' dress fiasco, we had a productive week."

Madeleine had gone with Ginger, Felicity, and Olivia to look for alternate dresses but hadn't had any luck. They searched as many stores as they could, given the busy holiday. Either there weren't enough dresses of the right size, there weren't enough dresses in the right color, or none of the dresses worked at all.

"That reminds me, Lisa texted to say the lady from the yellow house really liked us."

A high-pitched squeal escaped Madeleine's lips. "Really?"

"Yes." A.J. chuckled. "Don't get too excited though. We still have to go through the whole process of making an offer and passing inspection."

"I'm sure we'll be fine. That's exciting." Madeleine grinned out the window. She kicked off her tennis shoes and pulled her feet into a cross-legged position.

Packing A.J.'s meager possessions wouldn't be challenging. And she was confident they'd find buyers for his property in Shady Springs. Now that they had a house lined up, the move should be relatively straightforward.

"One less thing to worry about, huh?" A.J. winked at her.

She blew out a breath. "It's about time."

For a while, she leaned against the car window, watching trees and fields fly by.

"A.J.?"

"Hmm?"

"Do you think God is trying to prevent this wedding from happening?"

He pulled his head back suddenly. Thankfully, his hands remained steady on the wheel. "What makes you say that?"

"Oh, I don't know." Sarcasm laced every word. "The invitations were ruined, the wedding date had to be changed, the bridesmaids' dresses are all wrong, my mom has been hounding me about the budget, and I don't even know who to ask to walk me down the aisle."

A.J. quirked his head to the side as soon as she gave the last reason. "What do you mean?"

"I don't know if I should ask my mom or my dad to walk me down the aisle."

Still gripping the wheel with one hand, A.J. reached over to squeeze hers. He glanced her way with a sympathetic expression.

She didn't have to go on—A.J. knew everything she'd been through—but she kept talking. "I don't want to hurt Dad's feelings. But my mom is really the one who raised me."

They drove another moment in silence. Madeleine loved that A.J. didn't try to fill the air with words. He simply waited for her to speak again.

"What do you think I should do?"

"I think we should pray about it. And maybe you should sit down with them and have a conversation about this."

He was right. She knew he was right. But a serious conversation with her parents would be challenging. It would likely dredge up old issues. She groaned.

"Can I say one more thing?" A.J. squeezed again with his right hand before placing it back on the wheel.

"Uh-huh."

"I don't think God is trying to prevent this wedding." He gave a small smile, quickly catching her gaze. "You're a *gift* from God. I couldn't imagine a more perfect wife for myself."

"I couldn't imagine a more perfect husband." Her heart squeezed. She wished he wasn't driving so she could give him a kiss right then. Better to wait for the next pit stop.

"Planning a wedding is challenging, no matter what. Planning the *perfect* wedding is definitely going to be difficult." His smile was teasing—and adorable—even if she didn't think his joke was particularly funny.

She didn't have long to dwell on her irritation because A.J. asked to pray for her right then and there. A peace settled over her as he spoke to God about their wedding and their marriage. She still had so many decisions to make, but at least she had the comfort that only came from trusting in God. And she had a pretty great man by her side.

* * *

Interview with Arthur and Ginger Young

A.J.: How long have you two been married?

    Ginger: You don't know?

A.J.: …

Arthur: Your age plus five years, son.

A.J.: Do you know how old I am?

Arthur: ...

Madeleine: Thirty-two years of marriage. That's wonderful!

A.J.: What's your secret? How did you last this long?

Arthur: What are you trying to say?

    Ginger: Artie, hush.

Madeleine: What advice do you have for a young couple who wants to have a long marriage exactly like you?

Ginger: Humility and patience

Arthur: The right partner.

Madeleine: Aw. You two are so sweet.

A.J.: But you can stop kissing now. Thank you.

Arthur: The most important advice is to pray every day. Go to God with your troubles and let Him guide you.

Ginger: And we wouldn't be where we are today without the other Christian couples who've mentored us.

Arthur: We've been blessed with lots of good friends at church.

Ginger: And our parents.

Arthur: Yes, they've taught us a lot over the years.

Madeleine: I hope we can learn a lot from you too.

Ginger: Thank you, sweetie.

A.J.: Me too.

Arthur: What other questions do you have?

A.J.: I'm going to skip the questions about showing affection … Okay, here's a good one. How do you see your lives twenty years from now?

Arthur: I hope I get even better at communicating and giving grace.

Ginger: And I hope I learn to listen with an open mind. I want to always assume the best from you, Artie.

Arthur: In twenty years, I think our marriage will be better than ever.

Madeleine: Wow, I love that.

A.J.: Okay, you guys. I know you're not kissing, but you can stop making heart eyes at each other. Gross.

DECEMBER

Gustosa didn't open until noon, but the catering coordinator had agreed to meet her that morning to finalize the menu for the wedding reception.

Despite the complete disaster that was her engagement party, Madeleine had really loved the restaurant they'd eaten at. Now that she knew Arthur was allergic to pine nuts, they could avoid the pesto. She didn't want *another* visit to the ER with him.

Pulling into the parking lot, Madeleine spotted her dad's red sedan. As far back as she could remember, he'd gravitated toward bright crimson vehicles. It was one of the comforting connections to her childhood that had remained the same.

"Hey, Dad." Since Dad was the only other family member with a flexible schedule, he'd volunteered to help out this morning.

"Hi, Maddy-Maddy-Bo-Baddy." Dad pulled her into a hug, and she breathed in the scent of his cologne and spearmint gum.

Gustosa was decked out for Christmas. Even though the dining room wouldn't open for a few more hours, holiday music played over the speakers. Bright green, white, and red balls hung from the ceiling, matching the Italian flags perched on the front table.

The exposed brick, bright lights, and modern finishes of the restaurant made Madeleine's heart sing. But the garlic and butter smells coming from the kitchen were even more appealing.

"We're here for a meeting with Steve," Madeleine said to the first person she found, a young woman in a black uniform.

"Come on back. I'll show you to his office."

She led them through a back hallway to a series of doors. Tapping on one, she opened it for them. "Here you go."

"You must be Madeleine Mullins." A young man in a collared shirt stood to shake her hand.

"Hi. This is my dad, Henry." Madeleine held out her arm, indicating her father.

Steve shook his hand as well, then they all settled into their respective seats.

"I've already talked to Madeleine a little on the phone, but let me show both of you our menu of catering options."

He handed them each a stapled packet. There was a page of heavy hors d'oeuvres options and a page of full dinner options. Another page gave pricing for levels of service.

"We can provide anything from a buffet to full table service."

Dad's eyes widened a little more as he read over each page.

"Did you want to consider the appetizers?"

"A.J. really loves their lasagna …" She trailed off, hoping Dad would catch her meaning. Of all days, she didn't want to skimp on her wedding day. "I was thinking maybe the lasagna and the fettuccine alfredo would be popular. Or was there something you might prefer?"

Dad puckered his lips as he read over the menu again. "Those both sound good. Did you talk to Mom and A.J. already?"

They both knew she was meeting with the restaurant today. She hadn't yet disclosed any prices with them.

"How many people are you expecting at the wedding?" Steve asked. His hands were folded on the desk in front of him, and he watched them with a pleasant expression on his face.

"We haven't gotten all of our RSVPs in." They still hadn't heard from Great-Uncle Lew, as well as half the invited guests. "But we're expecting close to one hundred."

"Each of our pasta and salad trays serves about ten."

"Which means we'll need to multiply every price by ten," Dad said, still scanning the menu.

"And we do charge tax as well as a standard gratuity," Steve added, his smile still fixed in place.

"Right."

That meant she needed to add another thirty percent to the price. But how much was that price exactly? She was never as strong in her mathematical skills as other subjects in school. Mom was the practical, logical, mathematical one in the family. Which was why Madeleine had brought her father.

Who could put a price on the happiest day of her life? Not Madeleine. And she hoped her dad would feel the same.

As much as she loved the idea of full table service, she didn't want to *completely* drain her parents' bank account. She could reign it in a little. "How about a buffet with pasta and salad for one hundred? Maybe two or three options for people?" She and Steve picked their three most popular pastas—lasagna included. And the most popular salad.

"What about the tossed salad?" Dad asked.

Madeleine checked the menu. It was a few dollars cheaper, per tray, to get the tossed salad instead of the Caesar. "I thought you liked Caesar."

Dad nodded slowly as he chewed on his lip. "Okay."

"We do require a deposit of fifty-percent today to reserve your date. And we ask for full payment no later than fourteen days out from the event."

Steve turned to his computer to print the contract and the bill.

With a moment of privacy, Dad looked Madeleine in the eyes. "Is this what you really want?"

The smallest pang of guilt tugged at her, but she pushed it down. "Yes." This was simply the cost of feeding one hundred people. He should be glad she wasn't asking for a steak dinner and a string quartet like one of her college friends.

Dad leaned to the side to pull his wallet from his back pocket.

With the payment finalized, Steve outlined the contract for them. "You can make menu changes or change the head count up to the fourteen-day mark. Cancellations must be made thirty-six hours in advance except in the case of severe weather and will still require a thirty-percent cancellation fee."

Madeleine signed and dated each line, then took her copy of the contract. "Thank you so much, Steve."

"Thank *you*. And congratulations."

Walking out of the restaurant, Madeleine linked her arm in her dad's. "It sure feels great to check that off the list."

Dad smiled at her. "I'm glad."

"Thank you, Dad."

"Anything for you, Maddy."

$\mathcal{M}$adeleine had just about exhausted all other options when she finally went to Julie Ortega. She should've contacted her sooner, but she hated to ask for favors.

"Julie, I have a big problem I hope you can help with."

"Hello to you too." Julie laughed as she hugged Madeleine. "What can I do for you?"

Julie led Madeleine through the entrance of the chic bridal salon she managed. Madeleine had purchased her dress there but figured she couldn't find bridesmaids' gowns on such short notice.

"I need bridesmaids' dresses. The ones I ordered look completely different in-person." Madeleine's lip stuck out in a pout.

Julie tilted her head, giving her a sympathetic look as her dark ponytail hung to the side. "That happens sometimes, unfortunately."

"I should've come to you first, but I didn't think there would be any point since the wedding is in a few weeks."

"The seventeenth, right?" Julie had been one of the responsible people who actually got their RSVPs in on time. She clucked her tongue. "No, I'm afraid that's not enough time unless we find something on the sale rack. But let's go look just in case."

Madeleine followed her friend to the back of the store. A short rack with mismatched dresses sat in a corner. Without even rifling through the dresses, she could tell none of them were the right color. "I'd love a dark red or burgundy. Although a navy blue or metallic color might work." A quick look showed they were fresh out of those colors.

Disappointed, Madeleine turned to her friend. "What do you think I should do?"

Julie's golden honey skin creased as she frowned in thought. Then she gasped. "Oh, wait!" Her eyebrows lifted and she grabbed Madeleine's hand. "Come up to the front. I think I have a business card in my desk drawer."

Madeleine followed close behind, watching Julie's shiny hair whip back and forth. They stepped through a glass door into Julie's office. The space was brightly decorated in pink, green, and yellow.

"Here." Julie handed her a business card. "This is where we take any dresses that have imperfections or are returned but unsellable."

The blue card read "Beautiful Lives." Underneath was an address for a location in Fayetteville.

"They're a boutique resale shop that benefits women's charities. And they have people donate really nice wedding dresses. I bet we could find some nice bridesmaids dresses too."

We? "You'd go with me?"

Julie's smile was warm. "Of course. Between the two of us, I bet we can find something that will work."

Madeleine had to wait for Julie to take her lunch break, so she grabbed a coffee at a nearby shop and checked her phone.

Pulling open the bridesmaids' text thread, she sent a quick message.

> I might have a lead on some bridesmaids' dresses. I'll send pictures if I find something good.

Madeleine sipped at her gingerbread latte. The air had grown colder, but not so much that she couldn't enjoy the December sunshine on the patio of the coffee shop.

She really should start Christmas shopping. Most years, she tried to make gifts by hand for close friends and family. This year, she'd have to shell out some cash. She might have to actually ask people what they wanted.

While Madeleine still held her phone, she checked her running list of tasks.

- Finalize flower order
- Schedule the last counseling session with Sam
- Find a ring for A.J.
- Buy bridesmaids' presents.

Staci had talked her into a getaway at a vacation rental in Branson, Missouri the weekend before the wedding. A few days before the trip, she planned to pack up the last of her things still at her mom's place in Kansas City. Now that her parents were back together, Mom was selling her house and moving to Fayetteville. She'd been pestering Madeleine to go through boxes, but who had time for that?

> Can't wait!

Jenna, her college roommate, replied to her earlier text.

Let me know if it doesn't work out and you
want me to make something out of duct tape
and tulle!

Staci wrote.

Madeleine laughed.

Checking the time, she stood and walked to her car. She hoped Julie knew what she was talking about and this place wasn't a bust. She didn't want to think about what kind of dress Staci might come up with if left to her own devices.

* * *

Beautiful Lives was cuter than Madeleine imagined when she thought of a resale thrift store. Coffee and cookies greeted shoppers at the front door. A display of styled outfits in a unifying theme of creams and whites sat in the middle of the main floor.

If it weren't for displays with information about each charity the shop supported and large signs with sale prices, Madeleine might have assumed she was in an upscale boutique.

"This front room has their featured outfits."

Madeleine followed the direction Julie was pointing and saw a small room full of red and green holiday clothing. No tacky Christmas sweaters here—only sequined cocktail dresses and faux fur wraps.

"But we might find more options with the dresses." Julie gestured across the shop to another small room. Madeleine could even see some wedding dresses, just like Julie had said.

"Let's start there."

Each woman grabbed half a cookie before crossing the store to the dress area.

"Do you know what size each of your bridesmaids wear? And how many do you have?"

"There's only four. And they shared their measurements with me." Madeleine pulled up the note with their information on her phone.

"I'll start over in the smalls and you start in the larges."

Splitting up, Madeleine and Julie searched for the colors Madeleine thought might work with her wedding decor. Thankfully, she'd remembered to bring a sample wedding invitation to match the exact shades she'd painted. Before long, she had a stack of dresses weighing down her arm.

"Can I start rooms for you two?" A young blonde woman who looked to be in her early twenties poked her head around the doorframe.

"Yes, please!" Julie handed over her dresses with a smile. "You can put them under 'Madeleine.'"

"We're actually searching for bridesmaids' dresses."

The young woman's eyes lit up. "How fun! If you let me know what you're looking for, maybe I can help you out."

Madeleine handed over her invitation and explained her dilemma. "The wedding is coming up really soon. A little over two weeks." Her heart stuttered every time she said those words. But it was true. Time marched on, whether she was ready or not. "We ordered dresses, but they were all wrong." Madeleine showed a picture on her phone.

By the time she'd finished explaining her situation, two more women had gathered around. The first blonde took her stack of dresses and piled them on top of Julie's. "I bet we can find something for you. I'll hang these up in the dressing room."

One of the women looked to be a little older than Madeleine's parents. She wore her gray hair to her chin and dressed in slacks and a cardigan. "Did I hear you say you're looking for bridesmaids' dresses?" Her green eyes sparkled as she turned to the girl beside her. "I'm going to go look through the clothes we recently got in. I have a *God* feeling about this."

"Ooh!" The young woman she spoke with clasped her hands.

She turned to Madeleine and Julie as her coworker walked away. "Can I help you look through the last of the dresses in here?"

They combed through every single item hanging on the racks in the room. Madeleine almost wished she'd looked here first for her wedding dress. Some of them were gorgeous. Though she was still perfectly enamored with the gown she'd purchased from Julie's store.

"I think that's it. Let's look through everything we pulled."

Madeleine followed the young woman to a dressing area in the back of the store. Shelves of shoes lined one wall, with benches beside them. On the other side of the room were curtained fitting areas where women could try on their selections. A few floor-length mirrors dotted the room.

On a small rack were all the dresses Julie and Madeleine had chosen.

"Do you mind if we group these by color?"

"No problem." The employee beside her shrugged.

With Julie's help, they sorted all of the dresses into burgundies, navies, and metallic shades. There were a few great options, but not enough of one color in all the right sizes.

"Can we mix and match?" Julie asked.

"Do you think it would look okay?" Madeleine tilted her head and squinted at the outfits arrayed before them.

"Not really. But what other options do we have?"

Just then, a door in the back Madeleine hadn't noticed burst open. The woman who'd said she was going to look for more dresses came through with something over her arm.

Her bundle was covered in the kind of plastic that came from a dry cleaner, but the fabric looked like it might be a dark red.

"I remember seeing these dresses yesterday. We had a group of ladies from a church volunteering with us, and they prayed over the clothes we got. They asked God to bless our ministry and to bless the women who would get these clothes." She hung four plastic clothing bags on the rack. "I think God wants you to have these. They were donated after a wedding last week."

Madeleine pulled the first plastic covering off and gasped. Tears sprang to her eyes.

"Julie, look."

It was the dress. The exact same dress she'd picked out and knew she couldn't afford. How had it happened?

But she knew, of course.

God, I'm sorry I thought you were trying to prevent my wedding to A.J. I've been growing more and more discouraged with every setback. Maybe all this time you've been preparing me for something even better.

Julie helped uncover each of the four dresses, but Madeleine already knew in her heart that they were going to be perfect.

"They're going to need to be altered, I'm sure." Julie pulled the fabric of one of the dresses taut, examining it thoroughly. "And I can see a seam that needs to be repaired."

"Do you have anyone at your store who could help with alterations on short notice?"

"Yes." Julie grinned at her. "Me."

"Are you sure?" Blessings on blessings! Julie had become such a good friend, even though they'd only known each other a little over a year. "I know how busy you are."

Julie waved her off with one hand. "I can't promise it'll be perfect, but I can get it done quickly."

"Okay." Madeleine squealed. "I'll take all four of them."

"Can I pray for you? Would that be okay?" The woman in the red cardigan smiled, and Madeleine found herself holding back tears again.

"Of course."

She prayed for the upcoming wedding and for the preparations ahead.

"But God, we know most of all that the marriage itself is the important part. All of this wedding stuff is nothing compared to the life they'll live together. We pray that their marriage would glorify You above all."

Something in Madeleine rankled at that prayer. She *knew* the marriage was important. But wasn't that the whole point of the wedding? To start her marriage off on the right path? To show everyone how beautiful their union would be?

She tried not to let the prayer of a well-meaning stranger bother her. But her irritation lingered long after she'd paid her bill and said goodbye.

a.J. had almost forgotten about Christmas. In all the rushing around looking for houses, making honeymoon arrangements, and writing exams, his favorite holiday had snuck up on him.

But no one escaped Christmas at the mall.

A.J. held Madeleine's hand as they skirted around a line of children and parents. It snaked all the way from the food court, past the stalls selling sunglasses and stuffed animals, all the way to a large display with a jolly Santa sitting on a golden throne.

Teenaged elves and a photographer shuttled kids through the line as quickly as possible. Teary babies, anxious parents, and restless toddlers all mingled while a man played a medley of holiday music on the piano in the atrium.

Past the crowds, A.J. and Madeleine came to an intersection with a map of the shopping center.

"Which way should we go first?" A.J. asked. They'd each come with a Christmas list but had one big goal in mind.

"Let's pick out your ring." Madeleine squeezed his fingers. "That's the most important part. I can always order everyone a matching fleece blanket."

"What about one of those blankets with a picture on it?" He grinned down at her. "We could get one with our wedding picture and blow it up real big on a blanket."

Madeleine laughed, and the sound thrilled his heart more than any Christmas carol. "I don't think we'll get our photos back in time." She winked at him. "Maybe next year."

They found a jewelry store on the map and walked toward it hand-in-hand.

"Hello, how can I help you?" A man in a crisp black suit and slicked brown hair smiled at them as they walked in.

Did they radiate newly engaged happiness? The jeweler came toward them like they were a beacon.

"We're looking for wedding rings."

"Oh? Congratulations." The salesman's gaze flicked to Madeleine's left hand.

"It's for me." A.J. waggled the fingers of his left hand at the man.

If he was disappointed to be missing out on a lucrative sale, he didn't let on. He simply straightened his collar and motioned them to an area to their left. "Let me show you our selection of men's wedding bands." They turned to a display case against the side wall of the store. Bright lights reflected off bands of gold, silver, and all kinds of metals A.J. couldn't immediately recognize.

"Do you know what color or what metal you like?"

A.J. scanned the rainbow of rings before him. He'd always assumed he'd have a gold band like his dad, but he'd never realized how many options there were.

"I have a white gold band," Madeleine suggested. "Would you like something to match mine?"

"That could be nice." A.J. nodded, stuffing his hands in his pockets.

The salesman gestured to a section of the display. "We also have a selection of tungsten. These rings are virtually indestructible. It's especially good if you're frequently working with your hands."

"Oh, A.J., That sounds perfect for you."

He didn't want to burst her bubble, but he had to say it. "I don't know that I'll be working with my hands much in theology school."

Again, hardly a reaction from the jeweler. Merely a slight rise of the eyebrow and a pleasant smile.

"I think I'd like to stick with something simple." A.J. pointed to the plain bands in the corner of the glass case.

"If I know you, you're not going to let school keep you from working in the yard and fixing up the house." She wrapped her fingers around his elbow. "You'll always be working with your hands, even if it's not your job anymore."

"Would you like to try any of the rings on?" the jeweler asked.

"Can we look at that tungsten ring with the pattern and the white gold band with the diamonds?" Madeleine pointed to the case while the jeweler worked to pull out the rings she selected.

They had four boxes out on the counter.

"Let me see that plain tungsten ring, the white one. And the polished titanium ring too."

One by one, A.J. tried on the rings they selected. He held out his hand for Madeleine to see one of the patterned designs she'd picked out.

"That looks really nice on you."

"I don't know." He grimaced. "It doesn't look like me."

"I like this one." He pointed to another ring. Despite Madeleine's frown, he continued. "It's tungsten, which is cool, but it looks like a regular ring."

"Are you sure?" Madeleine's gaze searched his.

"Yes, I'm very sure."

"We're not able to resize tungsten, so let me make sure I have your exact size." The salesman held out a band with several rings of all different sizes. He had A.J. try them all on until one fit just right.

"I'll go write this down at the register and get you checked out."

When all was said and done, they left the store with a receipt and an appointment to come back and pick up his ring.

"We're going to be cutting it a little close." Madeleine frowned at the date on the receipt. They might not get the ring until the fifteenth, two days before the wedding.

"They said they'll call if it comes in sooner," A.J. reassured her. "That's another good reason to get a simple design—we're more likely to get it quickly."

As Madeleine tucked the receipt into her purse, her frown faded away. "Where to next?" She lifted the corners of her mouth in an almost smile.

They both had quite a bit of family to shop for and agreed to meet back in the food court for coffee—hot cocoa for A.J.—in two hours.

When A.J. returned to the agreed upon spot, he didn't have nearly as many bags as Madeleine. Between the bookstore and the gadget store, he'd checked off almost every gift from his list. From Madeleine's face, it looked like she'd had a more stressful shopping trip.

"I already ordered you a latte. It'll be ready soon." A.J. pointed to the nearby coffee stall before taking some of Madeleine's sacks to set on the table. "Looks like you were productive."

"Thank you." Madeleine sighed as she plopped into the seat across the table. Pushing aside some of the bags, she made a window through which they could see each other. "I forgot how exhausted I get after a day of shopping at the mall."

"It's been a while for me too." A.J. racked his brain but couldn't remember the last time he'd been to a mall. A few years at least.

The barista called out his name, and A.J. went to collect their drinks. He paused a moment, enjoying the medley of Christmas tunes coming from the piano nearby.

"Chestnut latte for you. Peppermint hot cocoa for me." He handed Madeleine the hot cups and slid into his seat.

The creamy chocolate warmed his belly. A.J. licked cool whipped cream from his top lip. "Mm." He set the drink back on the table. "How's yours?"

"Delicious." Madeleine sighed. "I love Christmas food."

She took another sip before returning her cup to the table. "Are you happy with the ring we picked out?"

"Yes."

"Because I really want you to like what you get."

"Why do you want me to pick out an expensive ring so badly?" Why didn't she believe him when he said he wanted a simple ring? Elaborate jewelry wasn't his style.

"It's not the cost." Madeleine's brow creased.

"What is it then?" A.J. searched her face.

"I feel like nothing is going the way I hoped."

"Didn't you just find the exact bridesmaids' dresses you wanted?" A.J. had been blown away by her story. He hoped that experience might make Madeleine calm down a little.

"I did. But there's still so much left to do and I'm afraid this wedding isn't going to be how I pictured at all."

He reached for her hand across the table. Her fingers were soft and warm from the heat of her coffee cup.

"From the time I was little"—Madeleine let her gaze drift up —"I had this image in my head of how I wanted my wedding day to look. I collected magazines and saved pictures online. Later, when I got older, I got to attend lots of my friends' weddings. Each time I solidified this dream in my head." She tapped her temple.

"What is it that you want?"

"I want magic." She sighed. "Twinkle lights and soft music

and candles and flower petals. Delicious cake and gorgeous dresses and a handsome groom."

"You've got that one covered." He squeezed her fingers and wiggled his eyebrows playfully.

She squeezed back and flashed a grin. "I love you so much. I'm excited to get married, even though I know everyone thinks we're rushing. Our parents and friends have all told us we should wait."

"We've been dating a while now."

"Yes, but we only met a little over a year ago."

He hesitated. He didn't want to ask the next question, but he had to. "Do you want to postpone the wedding?"

"No." She shook her head sharply.

"Then forget what other people think. This wedding isn't about them, it's about us."

"Okay. I just want to make sure you're happy. I don't want to sacrifice or skimp, just because we're doing things quickly." She bit her lip, and he reached across the table to rest his hand on her cheek.

He tilted his head to the side and smiled at Madeleine. Her light brown waves caught the light. Her cheeks flushed pink, and he brushed her soft skin with his thumb. "This wedding is going to be perfect, because it's ours. We don't need anything else."

As they walked out of the mall, A.J. carrying all of his bags and half of Madeleine's, the sounds of "Winter Wonderland" serenaded the shoppers. If only they could get married by a snowman like the couple in the song and have the whole wedding over with.

17

*E*ither she had a stomach bug, or Madeleine was dreading this wedding shower more than she'd anticipated. She'd only been a guest of honor a handful of times in her life, and never at the Shady Springs Church.

Only a little over a year ago, she'd refused to step foot in this building. After the fallout from her parents' separation and the unkind words of certain church members, she dreaded walking through the doors of *any* church building.

"You're fine. You like these ladies now. It's no big deal." Madeleine exhaled slowly.

Once she'd been hired by Aunt Clara to paint a mural here, she was forced to face the ghosts of her past. She'd realized they were not as terrifying as she'd built them up to be.

Time to step out in faith again.

Clutching a basket of hostess gifts, she pushed open the door to the fellowship hall.

And nearly walked into a large round table covered with pictures of her and A.J.

"Hey, there!" Aunt Clara came from across the room to give her a hug. "The woman of the hour."

Madeleine accepted the hug, then held out the basket. "I have some hostess gifts to pass out."

"Ooh! Let's bring these to the kitchen."

As they walked through the room, Madeleine glanced around. A few rectangular tables lined the wall, draped with white and lace tablecloths. One held a large bowl of pink punch and dozens of glass teacups. Another was stacked with trays of tiny sandwiches and cookies. A third table was set up in the middle of the room, next to two chairs. Already, a small mound of wrapped presents rested on top of it.

"Madeleine's here." Aunt Clara announced as she pushed her through to the kitchen.

Mom and Nancy Jones were there, as well as Susan Patterson and Julie Ortega.

"Congratulations." Julie enveloped Madeleine in a hug.

"Thank you." Madeleine, still holding the basket, wrapped one arm around Julie's middle. "I have gifts for you."

The ladies murmured their appreciation as she set the basket of goat milk soap and lotion on the kitchen island. Mom hung back next to Madeleine while the others selected their favorite scents.

"How are you feeling? Are you excited?" Mom nudged Madeleine's side with her elbow.

Madeleine shrugged. Despite the warm welcome and familiar faces in the kitchen, her stomach hadn't settled.

Only moments after each lady picked a hostess gift and the last napkin had been artfully arranged on the refreshments table, the first shower guests started trickling in through the doors. A whole ten minutes early.

"You sit over here." Aunt Clara directed Madeleine to one of the two chairs in the front. "And I'll sit next to you." Clara held a notebook and pen.

Madeleine shifted in her seat, tugging the wrinkles out of her skirt.

Julie appeared at her side. "Would you like some food?"

"No, thank you." Her stomach growled in betrayal, but Madeleine couldn't bear the thought of eating right now. "But I'd love something to drink."

"Sure thing." Julie glided over to the punch bowl and filled a cup with a liquid the color of bubblegum.

She brought the punch and a dainty napkin to Madeleine with a smile.

"Thank you." Madeleine took a sip. The syrupy liquid was thick with sherbet and stuck in her throat. She gave a polite nod before setting the cup in her lap.

Julie walked back over to the refreshments table. The other hostesses scattered through the room.

Susan rested her hand on Madeleine's shoulder. "How about we go ahead and start opening the gifts? I think it's going to take a while."

They both turned to the growing stack of presents on the table beside them.

Aunt Clara grabbed a box wrapped in silvery white paper. "Here, this is from me." She handed over the package then settled in with her notebook. "I'll keep track of the gifts for you."

After placing her teacup on the floor under her chair, Madeleine slid a finger under the wrapping paper.

Oohs and *aahs* rang out from the ladies sitting in the chairs fanned out in front of Madeleine. She showed them the box, a set of knives and a knife block. The only reason she knew they were good quality was because of the research she'd done before registering.

"Thank you, Aunt Clara." She also knew they were on the expensive side and a generous gift—especially for someone on a teaching salary.

"You're welcome, dear. Here's the next one."

Susan came to take the box of knives and Madeleine accepted the gift sack from Clara.

While about two dozen ladies looked on—and chatted and nibbled at treats—Madeleine opened each gift. There were monogrammed towels from Sam, a handmade wooden cutting board from the Pattersons, and a set of placemats from Julie.

"You have no idea how much we needed these," Madeleine called across the room to Julie, handing the placemats to Susan. Some of the butterflies in her stomach had flown away, and she actually found herself laughing, thinking about using paper towels under the plates at A.J.'s house.

She took another bag from Clara.

Some of the presents were off-registry, but Madeleine found herself appreciating the thoughtful handmade gifts. Maybe she didn't need a crocheted set of holiday kitchen towels, but she'd remember the woman who gave them to her every year.

Aunt Clara handed her a gold gift sack sprinkled with snowflake designs.

"That's from me," Nancy called out.

With each square of tissue paper removed, Madeleine could more clearly see blue gingham cloth. She unfolded the cloth to reveal an apron with her name embroidered in cursive across the front.

"You might actually have to start cooking now." Clara elbowed her playfully.

Mom's loud laugh rang out from across the room.

"Thanks, you two." Madeleine rolled her eyes.

"There's more." Nancy cupped her hands to be heard over the giggling women around her.

Reaching in a second time, Madeleine found another—larger—apron. This one had "A.J." in bold print.

"Perfect." This time Clara's voice held sincerity. "Now you can learn together."

Madeleine smiled, clutching the apron to her chest. "Thank you, Nancy, I love them."

Her heart full to bursting, she quick-stepped over to Nancy to hug her neck. Madeleine blinked back the stinging in her eyes.

After twenty more minutes of opening presents and thanking each giver, Susan volunteered to pray a blessing over Madeleine and A.J.

"Each of the gifts given today represents a person who loves Madeleine and A.J. But, Lord, we know you love them even more. We pray you would bless their marriage and that you would empower us to support and care for them in their life together."

For years, Madeleine could only shake her head in disbelief when Aunt Clara talked about her church family. But now she understood. These women showed up for her. And Susan wanted the church to support her new marriage. She didn't know what exactly that might look like, but her heart swelled at the sentiment.

After the last "amen" was uttered, the ladies broke off into smaller groups and gravitated toward the door. Madeleine pulled out her phone to text A.J. He'd promised to come by with his truck after the shower, and she'd need all the help she could get carting these gifts away.

Looking up from her phone, Madeleine spotted Susan. She stepped closer to the woman and caught her arm.

"Thank you for that prayer. It was really beautiful."

"You're welcome." Susan smiled.

"And thank you for hosting this shower." Madeleine glanced at the gifts, now carefully stacked on a table by the door. "I'm a little overwhelmed."

Susan gave a sympathetic frown. "Sitting up there in the center of attention can be taxing."

"No." Madeleine shook her head. "That's not what I meant. I'm grateful. I feel so loved."

"You are loved." Susan's eyes wrinkled at the corners.

"That's what we're here for. Not only for the presents and the wedding, but later too. We'll be there to help you out."

Madeleine had so many questions about what that would look like. Would she ever be on the other side of this conversation, helping a young bride navigate her new marriage? She hoped God would bring her there someday, but for now the chasm between Madeleine and her future gaped too wide.

18

adeleine had never been to the Shady Springs Christmas parade, but from the buzz of excitement and the crowd gathered around the street, she must be the only one. The tradition had started after she and her mom had moved to Kansas City. According to her aunt, every year, the town would gather downtown and watch as trailers with light displays drove past. Different clubs from the school, community groups, and businesses put together floats. And the very last vehicle was always a fire truck with Santa and Mrs. Claus waving from the back.

She wasn't a huge parade person—all the loud sirens and diesel smells turned her stomach, but tonight was about supporting her family. Aunt Clara and the chemistry club had a float this year. Even if this wasn't her first choice of how to spend her evening, she was guaranteed to be entertained.

Madeleine's parents had come in for the weekend and met her and A.J. in front of the church building. They carried lawn chairs, fleece blankets, and travel mugs of cocoa to one of the last remaining open spots on the grass beside Main Street.

"I'm told our church building is one of the better spots to watch the parade." Madeleine placed her chair between Mom's and A.J.'s.

"It is," A.J. said. "Lots of people try to squeeze in toward the start of the parade by Mike's Diner, but there's more room to spread out here. The only downside—the dancing troupes are worn out and the band is tired of playing 'Jingle Bells' by the time they get to us."

They'd arrived early, per A.J.'s recommendation. As time wore on, his advice proved sound. Crowds of people showed up carrying cocoa, chairs, and glow sticks. Dad and A.J. eventually abandoned their chairs to keep watch from the sidewalk.

Madeleine sipped her cocoa from her seat. Let the guys get excited. She'd stay warm with her blanket and her hot beverage.

"Dad showed me the bill for the caterers," Mom said, keeping her voice low.

"Yeah?" What did Mom want her to say? The cost of food had been higher than she budgeted for, but Dad had paid for it with no problem.

"It was a lot more than we'd agreed on."

"I know it was high," Madeleine admitted, keeping her eyes on the street ahead. "But we have to serve dinner. The wording on the invitations and the timing of the ceremony—"

"If we're going to spend thousands of dollars on a full meal for everyone, we're going to need to cut from another part of the budget."

She whipped her head toward Mom. "What do you mean?"

"Maybe we could buy fewer flowers or cancel the videographer—"

At that moment, a loud siren sounded. Madeleine clapped her hands over her ears as a pair of police cars flashed their lights while driving slowly down the street. The parade had begun. Dad and A.J. joined them in their chairs.

Madeleine tried her best to enjoy the marching band and the pageant queens waving from convertibles. Every person in the parade wore some kind of Christmas sweater, hat, or costume. Bright lights flashed against the dark night, and loud festive music pumped through car speakers.

The spectacle brought smiles to everyone's faces, and children around her squealed with delight. But Madeleine's stomach grew sour. Mom's words rang louder than the drums.

How could Mom consider cutting flowers or the videographer? They were every bit as important as the food. She knew they didn't have the budget of a royal wedding, but she wanted the chance for this one to feel beautiful. Like the celebration it was.

Trailer after trailer rolled past, each with strings of colorful lights. Local businessmen and politicians waved and tossed flyers and candy.

"There's the chemistry club." Dad pointed.

Sure enough, a trailer full of teens wearing lab coats appeared behind the truck. Each kid held tubes and beakers full of luminous neon materials. At the center of the float was Aunt Clara. Madeleine couldn't tell if she'd teased her tresses to stand on end or if she wore a wig. Either way, her hair was a sight to behold. She looked like Albert Einstein's crazy twin sister.

Black lights illuminated the trailer, and Clara had constructed a laboratory of pipes and plywood around them. A large banner read "Shady Springs High Chemistry Club."

"Is this something they do every year?" Madeleine leaned close to A.J. to ask him.

"No," A.J. shouted back to her. "They talked her into it this year."

From the looks of it, Aunt Clara hadn't taken much convincing. Madeleine waved both hands to her aunt as the trailer continued on down the road.

Next came a dancing troupe of young girls dressed in elf and reindeer outfits. They marched down the street in time to a newer holiday song Madeleine had heard on the radio. A person inside an inflatable snowman suit followed behind them, throwing candy to the kids on either side of the street.

Although she'd been warned, Madeleine forgot to plug her ears before the fire truck made its way toward them. All the kids screamed and jumped up and down as if a famous rock star approached.

Santa and Mrs. Claus waved and blew kisses to the crowd while firefighters tossed peppermints.

With the crowds dwindling and the floats gone, peace returned. Except for the tight tension in Madeleine's chest.

She faced her mother. "I really want to serve dinner at the wedding reception."

Mom sighed. "I know, sweetie. Can we come up with a compromise?"

Madeleine nodded, her throat tight. What choice did she have?

"I want this wedding to be perfect for you too. But I can't give you money I don't have." Mom rested a hand on Madeleine's arm.

"I get it," Madeleine said softly. "But it's too late to find another restaurant."

"If you let us help out, I bet we can find something everyone's happy with. Dad said there were some less expensive options."

"Okay."

"And no more railroading Dad into paying large amounts of money." Mom leveled a sharp look her way.

Madeleine bristled. "Hey—"

"You know he'd do anything to make you happy. I'm officially revoking his credit card privileges until after this wedding is over."

"Fine."

"I'm glad we're in agreement."

Madeleine resisted the urge to roll her eyes and stomp her feet. In her heart, she knew Mom meant well. But this sure felt a lot like sabotage.

19

Would Madeleine ever see this house again?

She turned a circle around her childhood bedroom, trying to soak in all the memories.

After over a decade here, her mom was packing up the house in Kansas City and moving to Fayetteville in January, and Madeleine might never have a reason to come back. As much as she hoped to visit Kansas City frequently, she couldn't know for sure what the future might bring.

Mom had been so busy boxing items in the other rooms, she hadn't touched Madeleine's things. Pictures still hung on the walls. Stuffed animals rested on the bed. Trophies and ribbons lined the shelves above her desk.

She had her work cut out for her.

Over the course of the last year, Madeleine had slowly moved many of her things out of the Kansas City house and over to Shady Springs where she'd been living with her aunt. The closet only held a few formal dresses—all the art supplies had been cleared out.

Only keepsakes Madeleine couldn't bear to part with but couldn't bother to take with her remained in that bedroom.

"Here's how I've been organizing." Mom walked in with two boxes and a trash bag. Each had a label—*donate*, *trash*, or *keep*. Very straightforward.

"I can donate whatever you like when I take a load to the church." The congregation mom had joined when she started going back to church last year had a charity shop and food pantry. Madeleine felt better knowing anything she gave away would go to a good cause.

"Thanks, Mom."

"Let me know if you need anything." Mom took off down the hall to work on her own bedroom.

For over an hour, Madeleine sorted through her mementos and knick-knacks. The process wouldn't take so long, except she had to reminisce over every item before sorting it into one of the boxes.

With her desk cleared off, Madeleine turned to the bed. Underneath were some clear plastic totes full of memorabilia and old toys. She found a doll from her grandmother that would definitely be going to the *donation* box.

In the very back corner was a stack of binders and notebooks from grade school. She pulled them all onto the top of the bed. They made a loud thump as they sank several inches deep into her comforter.

And there, on the very top of the stack, was her old wedding planning binder.

It was dusty from years of neglect, but Madeleine was taken right back to her childhood when she opened the first page.

"Oh, wow," Madeleine whispered reverently. She lightly touched the faded magazine pictures and fabric samples with the tips of her fingers.

She laughed at a photo from the early 2000s of an orangey spray-tanned model wearing the glossiest lip gloss and the smokiest eye shadow. Some trends were best left in the past.

Flopping onto the bed, Madeleine lay on her stomach,

flipping the pages. Would Mom be mad she was spending so much time leafing through a binder full of outdated pictures and ideas she'd long since abandoned? This wasn't the most productive use of her time. Oh well.

Madeleine sucked in a breath when she came to the last page. She'd completely forgotten about this handkerchief. Her babysitter Emily had given it to her when she was a flower girl in her wedding. And later that evening, Emily's mother had given Madeleine this binder. Madeleine's initials were embroidered in pale blue in the corner. As gently as possible, she tugged the delicate fabric from the binder pocket and held it to her chest.

Capturing the magic she felt watching Emily get married was probably impossible. Every couple was different, and times and trends had changed considerably since then.

But Madeleine hoped her wedding to A.J. could be every bit as beautiful and special in its own way.

Should she keep the binder? Trash it? Madeleine folded the handkerchief and tucked it in her pocket. She held up the binder, briefly hovering over the *donate* box before letting it fall on the pile of trash.

All of the magazine clippings she'd thought were so important lost their significance over time. Only the handkerchief, with its special human connection, was valuable.

Madeleine thought back to her wedding shower. Each of the gifts she and A.J. received would help them in a practical sense, but their true significance lay deeper. What made each present special was the love it represented.

The mostly bare walls and shelves bore testimony to the impermanence of objects. What truly lasted were the memories and the love.

Mom and A.J. had been trying to tell her for weeks that the wedding wasn't important. Or, at least, not as important as she was making it out to be. Maybe it was time for Madeleine to start listening.

* * *

That night, over dinner, Madeleine shared her progress with her mom. "I've got the whole bedroom sorted. And tomorrow morning, I can clean out the bathroom and hall closet." She grinned, waiting for Mom's approval.

"That's great, Maddy. Thank you for all your hard work."

Madeleine chewed her food thoughtfully. She didn't really want to bring it up, but she knew they needed to talk about the wedding budget.

"I was able to get the wedding menu changed."

"Yes." Mom kept fishing for a bite of salad with her fork. They'd had a brief conversation over the phone about this. Mom already knew she'd cut back on the menu to save a little money.

"And I wanted to apologize."

Mom set her fork down, the bite of lettuce still on its tines. "What for, sweetie?"

"For talking Dad into the more expensive options. And for generally being difficult."

"Which time?" Mom laughed, but in a way that sounded more affectionate than mean.

"Specifically in the last couple months while we've been planning this wedding."

Mom raised her napkin to her face, dabbing at the corner of her lips before lowering her napkin back to her lap. "Planning a wedding is stressful."

"I know, but I think I'm losing sight of the big picture." Madeleine twirled her fork absentmindedly. "The wedding is supposed to be about A.J. and me getting married. Not about showing off or impressing anyone."

"Is that what you've been trying to do?"

"Not intentionally." Madeleine took another bite and chewed before finishing her answer. "I wanted to show to everyone how perfect A.J. and I are together. And I want to do it right, you know?"

Mom cocked her head to one side, but didn't speak.

"What would it say about us if we had a slap-dash thrown together wedding? What would that say about me as an artist? Or about our future as a couple?"

"Why does it all have to mean something? Can't you simply get married?" Mom asked.

"Not in this day and age." Madeleine shook her head. "Everything has to be personalized and photogenic. People want a viral video of the wedding dance or some cute thing the groomsmen do. Or have an Instagram-worthy photo backdrop. Or a glambot photo booth with amazing videos of the guests."

"What's a glambot?"

"Never mind." Madeleine slashed her fork through the air. Thankfully, no salad flew across the room. "That's not the point."

"What is?"

"I don't know. I think with social media and smartphones, everything has turned into a massive production. But weddings are the worst of all."

"But isn't that what you're saying? You want your wedding to display your relationship to the world?"

Madeleine let her head sink into her hands. "I don't know anymore."

"Maddy, no one is going to be coming to your wedding to judge you. And if you don't want to post anything on social media, your marriage to A.J. will be just as legitimate." Mom reached across the table to grab Madeleine's hands. "You only need to worry about what *you* and *A.J.* want. Not what anyone else will think."

Sometimes Madeleine resented the fact that her mom was

almost always right. But tonight it was reassuring. "Thanks, Mom."

"And when all this is said and done, I think you could make a pretty great modern art exhibit about the social pressures of weddings and the bride as a metaphor for … something."

Madeleine laughed. "Not a bad idea." But she hoped she'd be able to get more out of this experience than a metaphor. Why did getting married have to be so difficult?

20

A.J. wasn't sure how Madeleine's friends had managed to find such a cool house for their bachelor and bachelorette weekend, but he was pumped to be staying here for two nights. From the outside, the house appeared like a regular, two-story home. But inside, there was every amenity he could ever hope for on a vacation. A large kitchen opened up to a large dining table with room enough for all ten people staying. Around the corner was a living room with overstuffed couches and a large coffee table stocked with board games, puzzles, and cards. And along the far wall were tall windows overlooking the rolling hills of Branson, Missouri. He could even spot a roller coaster in the distance.

All of that plus their comfortable beds would have been enough, but there was more. Downstairs was a large game room with a pool table, pinball, and a skee-ball machine. Next door to that was a movie room with a large screen and long sectional sofa. Outside was a hot tub, a fire pit, a basketball hoop, and a mini golf range. Festive decorations sprinkled the house, with garlands draped around the stair rails and fireplace mantle and white lights lining the roof.

"Sweet!" Sounded like some of the groomsmen had arrived.

"Hey, Cole!" A.J. slapped his friend on the back in a hug. "Wait until you see the backyard."

A.J.'s groomsmen were a combination of friends from high school and college. He'd considered asking cousins but decided that was a minefield he'd like to avoid, since he didn't want to leave anyone out and risk upsetting his parents.

Two of his friends were bringing their wives, but Cole was still single and had come by himself from Tulsa.

"Want a soda? The bridesmaids stocked the fridge before we got here."

"Don't drink all my Dr. Pepper!" Staci's voice rang through the living room.

A.J. had briefly met Madeleine's friend when he'd gone with her to Kansas City. She was definitely an acquired taste. He was thankful he didn't have to see too much of her—outside of this weekend.

"How about if I just have one and you can have one too?" Cole took two cans from the fridge, handing one to Staci. "A.J.? You want anything?"

"No thanks."

The front door opened and three more people stepped inside —A.J.'s friends Trey and Brandon, with Brandon's wife Erin. The guys slapped backs and greeted each other, while Staci introduced herself to Erin.

"Come with me." Staci smiled at her. "I can give you a tour of the house."

"Let's all go explore," A.J. suggested. "I think Matt and Shelby won't get here until closer to dinner. And Madeleine and Jenna have been upstairs unpacking way too long."

The six of them trooped downstairs, oohing and aahing over the game room and theater, then cheering over the backyard.

"How did you find this place?" Erin asked Staci.

"They had a last-minute cancellation and I snatched it up." She laughed. "Branson is usually super busy around Christmas, so I was shocked."

"I can't wait to see the city all lit up. I've never been here in December." Madeleine sidled up to A.J., wrapping her arm around his waist. She radiated a calm he hadn't seen in her since before he'd proposed. Spending time with friends and away from the wedding planning must've been exactly what she needed.

The group decided to settle into their rooms and hang out by the fire pit before supper. A.J. and Brandon volunteered to start up the grill while Trey and Cole found logs for the fire pit. They'd all smell like smoke before the night was over, but A.J. didn't mind.

"How're you feeling? How's wedding planning going?" Brandon had been married to Erin for almost four years. They all met as kids in the junior high youth group, and Trey had come along later in high school.

What must it be like to be so young and already know who you wanted to spend the rest of your life with? A.J. didn't remember Brandon and Erin having any major relationship issues growing up. They always seemed to be the perfect couple.

"It's fine." A.J. shrugged. He didn't want to talk badly about Madeleine or act like he wasn't happy to be getting married. But he couldn't lie and say everything was going swimmingly either.

Brandon whistled. "I remember how stressed Erin and I were when we were getting married. And I think weddings get more and more over-the-top every time we go to one."

"We said we were going to keep things simple." A.J. pulled the cover off the gas grill. It looked like there was plenty of propane, but he'd be sure to stop by the store later to grab more. "But Madeleine wants everything to be just so. I wish I could help more but she doesn't want me to do anything."

"That's just how it is." Brandon shoved his hands in his

pockets, rocking on his feet. "Erin wanted everything to be a certain way for our wedding, and I just had to stand back and tell her how great it all was."

Madeleine wasn't normally a very fussy person. She was every bit as comfortable in paint-covered overalls as she was in a dress. But this wedding was bringing out the worst in her. How could he simply stand back and watch?

"Women have all these extra expectations. I guess sometimes they put it on themselves or sometimes society puts it on them." Brandon waved one hand back and forth in the air. "It's hard for guys to understand it all."

A.J. stared at his friend.

"I mean"—Brandon laughed—"that's what Erin tells me, at least."

Marriage had changed his friend, but on the whole it was for the better.

Once they'd finished grilling hamburgers and chicken breasts for everyone, they brought it inside to the kitchen. Madeleine and Jenna had set out trays of veggies and burger buns on the kitchen island, and everyone gathered around to fill their plates. Matt and Shelby walked in when they were almost all settled at the table, so A.J. took a break to take their bags and get them some dinner.

When everyone was finally settled at their places around the table, A.J. volunteered to say a prayer. He grabbed Madeleine's hand in his and squeezed. He smiled at each of the faces looking back at him. They were likely hungry and irritated that he was taking so long to start talking, but he didn't care. He took one more minute to soak in all the love he felt from their group of friends, and then he bowed his head.

Words couldn't fully express his gratitude for being there with a table full of friends and his future wife by his side. There had been many days when he doubted he'd ever get to this point.

But God had blessed him with every person at this table, even the ones he didn't know as well. Because they were here to celebrate Madeleine and him. He hoped they would continue to support their marriage for a long, long time.

21

$\mathcal{B}$ranson at Christmas was even better in person than in the pictures. Madeleine had visited the town before with friends or with her mom, but never during the holidays. The giant tree at Silver Dollar City, the music, the lights. It filled her with more happiness than she'd felt in a while.

Planning a wedding should make her happy. And sometimes it did.

When she thought about her future life with A.J. Or when she remembered how long she'd looked forward to the day when she'd finally be the one walking down the aisle, she was overcome with emotion. But most days, she was just ready to be done.

When Staci suggested taking a vacation with the wedding party a week before the wedding, Madeleine had thought she was crazy. Who had time—or money—for a trip like this while trying to get married? But then Staci told her they'd be splitting the bill and Madeleine and A.J. would only have to pay the cost of theme park tickets and food. With an offer like that, she could hardly refuse.

A.J.'s sisters and Jenna's husband hadn't been able to make

the trip, but with Matt's and Brandon's wives, there was an even number of guys and girls. Madeleine was getting to hear stories about A.J. in college and high school. It almost made up for all the stories Jenna and Staci were sharing about her.

The group spent the morning and early afternoon riding roller coasters and eating their fill of park food. They watched craftsmen blow glass ornaments and dip candles.

Walking under a canopy of lights, sharing cinnamon bread with A.J., Madeleine could forget about everything else.

When they got back from the park, everyone was too stuffed to eat dinner and decided to snack on popcorn and desserts that night.

The guys headed down to the game room. One of them mentioned watching a movie later.

With the main floor a bit quieter, the girls settled around the living room. Madeleine made herself a cup of tea and helped Jenna and Erin find ingredients for hot cocoa.

"Are you ready to get married in a week?" Staci asked when Madeleine was comfortably tucked into a corner of one of the couches, a throw blanket over her legs and a warm mug in her hands.

"Yes and no." Madeleine couldn't decide if she was more scared or excited. "We've checked almost everything off the list, but I know there's still so much that could go wrong."

"I remember being so ready to run off to Jamaica when I was getting married." Jenna settled on one of the couches across from Madeleine. "It all turned out beautifully though, and I'm so glad we put in the time and energy to make it a good day."

"Your wedding was perfect." Madeleine remembered Jenna's ceremony in a cathedral with light pouring through stained-glass windows and sounds of the string quartet floating in the air. The reception afterward in a nearby hotel had been over-the-top in a fun way. There was a live band, a four-course meal, and a chocolate fountain. The *pièce de résistance* was the towering white cake at the center of the room. It rose over the guests like a frosted castle gleaming under bright spotlights. And it tasted every bit as delicious as it looked.

Madeleine desperately wished she had the funds or the time needed to pull off a wedding as spectacular as Jenna's.

"Thank you, Madeleine." Jenna gave a half-pout, half-smile. Sort of condescending but sweet at the same time. "I was so happy to have you as one of the bridesmaids."

"What about you two? What were your weddings like?" Staci pointed to Erin and Shelby, now sitting between Madeleine and Jenna, at the couch opposite the fireplace.

"Ours was really small, but sweet." Shelby answered first. "We had it at my grandparents' house out in the country, so we had to keep it to close friends and family. But I was just happy to be marrying Matt."

"I know what you mean." Erin nodded. "That's all that really matters."

Erin took a sip of her hot cocoa before continuing. "I would change so many things about our wedding if I could."

"Like what?" Madeleine asked.

"Well, the person in charge of music, for starters. He kept repeating the same song over and over again when people were walking in because he couldn't figure out how to work the phone playing the music."

Madeleine and A.J. had worked together to pick meaningful songs for their ceremony, but she hadn't thought about who'd be running the sound system. What if they messed it all up?

"And then our flower girl tripped and fell on the way down the aisle."

"Aww, but flower girls and ring bearers messing up is cute." Staci spoke up.

"Not if she gets a carpet burn on her face and runs screaming to her mom." Erin laughed, but Shelby looked at her with raised eyebrows and a pout.

"Oh, she was fine by the time she got some cake." Erin waved her off.

Madeleine was glad now they'd decided not to have a flower girl or ring bearer. Wedding plans had been complicated already, and neither of them had any nephews or nieces or even a young enough cousin. Now she had one less thing to worry about.

"But by that point I didn't really care what happened, as long as I got to marry Brandon." Erin shrugged. "The wedding's not really the important part anyway."

"What do you mean?" Madeleine asked.

"It's the marriage that matters most."

"And the honeymoon!" Jenna giggled, and all the other women joined in.

"I forget," Shelby said as she turned to Madeleine. "Where are you going for your honeymoon?"

"A.J.'s organized the whole thing." Madeleine was thankful at least one aspect of wedding planning had been off of her plate. "We're going to stay at a house that his dad's friend owns."

The other women waited expectantly.

"Oh, um, we're going to New Orleans."

They all smiled then and started talking over each other.

"Wow!"

"That'll be so fun."

"Are you going to any art museums?" Jenna asked.

"Yes, but mostly I want to just walk around and listen to music."

"And eat beignets!" Shelby licked her lips dramatically.

"You're going to have a great time." Erin chimed in.

"And New Orleans should be nice too." Shelby laughed.

* * *

Interview with Brandon and Erin Porter

A.J.: How long have you been married?

Brandon: Four years.

Erin: And a half.

Madeleine: And how long did you date before that?

Erin: Eight years.

Brandon: And a half.

Madeleine: Wow, that's amazing.

A.J.: What's been the hardest part of married life so far?

Brandon: I think—and correct me if you think I'm wrong, here, Erin—I think the hardest part was adjusting to each other's quirks.

Erin: I agree. We'd been dating for so long, we thought we knew everything about each other.

Brandon: But I didn't know how long it took you to get ready in the morning.

Erin: And I didn't know that you snore during pollen season in the spring.

Brandon: I didn't know Erin liked to squeeze the toothpaste tube from the middle and rip open chip bags like an animal.

Erin: And I didn't know you have an aversion to putting your shoes away or taking out the trash.

A.J.: Okay. The little quirks have been the most difficult part?

Erin: So far.

Madeleine: What's the best part about marriage?

Erin: I get to hang out with my best friend every day.

Brandon: Sometimes I forget to call friends or hang out with anyone else because I'm having so much fun being at home with Erin.

Erin: It's like having a slumber party every night.

Madeleine: What was the first year like for you?

Erin: It was hard but good … Does that make sense?

Brandon: We had all those quirks to work through—and

we're still working through some of them—but it was what we'd been looking forward to for eight years.

Madeleine: And a half.

A.J.: What advice do you have for us?

Brandon: I'm really glad you're doing premarital counseling. That was helpful for us too. There's a lot you can't plan or anticipate. But we were able to talk about the big things beforehand.

Madeleine: Like what?

Erin: Like who we'd spend Christmas with or how many kids we wanted. Although—

Brandon: We'd pretty much figured that out in high school.

A.J.: Any other advice? Erin?

Erin: Remember to keep God at the foundation of your marriage. And pray for each other daily. It's a lot harder to be mad at someone when you're praying for them.

Brandon: And find a good church family. Even though we still live close to family, our young adults group at church has been a huge support for us.

Erin: We love you guys and are so excited for you!

22

A.J. was back at school the next Monday when he started getting text messages. The first was from Erin.

> Brandon has a fever today. Are you feeling okay?

Truth be told, he was feeling a little tired. He'd assumed that was the result of staying up too late with his friends all weekend. Lifting his hand to his forehead, he checked for a high temperature, but his skin felt normal.

> That was a fun weekend, but I'm exhausted now. Maybe we're getting too old for this.

That was from Trey.

A.J. wasn't worried until Madeleine called at the end of the day.

"Both Staci and Jenna are sick."

If Brandon, Trey, Staci, and Jenna were all ill, he couldn't chalk it up to coincidence and late nights anymore.

"How are you feeling?" A.J. asked. If Madeleine was sick, then he'd *really* need to start worrying.

"I'm okay, I think." She paused. "I don't know. I can't tell if I'm actually sick or just paranoid."

They both agreed to go to bed early that night and pray that everyone would feel better in the morning.

But the next morning, A.J. was worse. When his alarm blared at six o'clock, he fought every instinct telling him to hit snooze and go back to sleep. Pushing his body to sit up, he immediately regretted the choice. His head pounded and his muscles ached as if the entire Shady Springs track team had run over him the night before.

He should call in sick. And if he worked a normal job, he *would* call in sick. But calling in sick would mean writing lesson plans for a substitute and he couldn't … A sudden realization struck him. It was finals week. He *could* call in for a sub because his final exams were printed and ready to go on his desk.

"Ms. Bea, this is A.J. Young." His voice didn't want to cooperate and squeaked out raspy and weak.

"Hi, Mr. Young," the school administrative assistant answered. She always insisted on calling teachers by their last name, even though she was older than all of them. "You don't sound so good."

"I'm going to need a sub today. I've filled out the information on the website, but I wanted to let you know." Everything nowadays was funneled through an online service, which was supposed to save the school office time and effort, but he still had to call the front office. Seemed like about the same amount of work to him. "I left my tests for today on the desk, so it should be very straightforward. Would you let the sub in and tell him or her to call me if they need help with anything?"

"Sure thing." Teresa typed something on the other end. "What do you think it is?"

A.J. assumed she was asking about his illness. "I don't know, but everyone I spent time with over the weekend seems to be sick too."

"I hope we don't have something bad going around." She whistled. "All right, you get some rest and come back feeling better tomorrow. We want you better for the wedding this weekend."

The wedding. He only had four days to kick this bug. Should he tell Madeleine or would that make everything worse? No, she had enough to worry about right now, and that last phone call had drained him of all energy.

Slowly, he pulled his legs back into bed and rested his head on his pillow. Maybe rest was all he needed to feel better.

A sound pulled him from sleep. An insistent ring drilled into his head.

His phone.

"Who's calling me?" He patted the bed beside him until he located the vibrating device. Squinting at the screen, he made out Madeleine's name and photo.

He swiped to answer. "Hello?"

"I've had two more text messages from bridesmaids."

"What time is it?" He glanced over at his clock. Eleven-thirty. Normally, he'd be eating lunch right now—why Madeleine felt free to call.

"It's—wait." Madeleine's voice was laced with suspicion. "Why do you sound like you just woke up?"

A.J. rolled to the side and grabbed a pillow to prop under his arm. "Because I did."

Long pause.

"A.J. are you sick? Please tell me you're not sick."

"Do you want the truth?"

Something between a groan and a scream came out of her mouth. A.J. imagined she was about ready to pull out her hair. "You can't be sick. Why are you sick?"

"Either from my students or our friends this weekend. Who knows?"

"Have you been to the doctor?"

"I've been sleeping."

"Stay where you are. I'm picking you up."

He hadn't planned on moving from his spot on the bed, so he was happy to oblige. But he might nap while he waited.

A.J. opened his eyes again when he heard a key in the front door.

"A.J.? Are you in bed?"

Footsteps sounded in the hall.

"A.J.?" Madeleine's voice was quieter as she peered through the doorway. "Oh, you poor thing."

She padded across the carpet, perched on the bed, and held the back of her hand to his forehead.

"Oh!" She pulled her hand away. "You're burning hot."

"Your hand is cold." His voice came out petulant. She was going to make him stand up, and he was already irritated.

"Come on. Do you need to go to the bathroom? Brush your teeth?"

With Madeleine's urging, he went to the restroom, ran a toothbrush over his teeth and tongue, and added a hoodie over his shirt—to formalize the ensemble.

Madeleine took one of his arms and slung it over her shoulders, wrapping her arm around his waist. He didn't need quite that much help walking, but he wasn't going to complain about the free hug.

"Want me to drive?" He knew what she was going to say. He just wanted to see her reaction.

Madeleine turned to face him and pursed her lips. "Are you kidding me? I'd like to survive the day, thank you very much." She rolled her eyes for good measure, then opened the passenger door of her sedan and guided him inside. A.J. shivered involuntarily as he buckled his seatbelt. He missed the warmth of Madeleine's body, and his sweatshirt wasn't enough to fight off the cold air.

One of the many benefits of living in a small town was the

easy commute from his house to the doctor's office. In only a few minutes, they were pulling into Dr. Thomas's parking lot.

The waiting room was busy for a Tuesday morning, and they had to wait a while to be called back. A.J. rested his head on Madeleine's shoulder while she answered emails and solved crossword puzzles on her phone. The front desk of the waiting room was decorated with tinsel, and paper honeycomb decorations hung from the ceiling tiles. An aluminum tree stood in one corner, lit with a rainbow of colored lights. It reminded him of his grandmother's house.

"I'll wait out here for you," Madeleine offered when his name was called.

A.J. would need to add her as his emergency contact on a day when he wasn't running a temperature.

"You tested positive for flu A," Dr. Thomas told him thirty minutes later. "I can put you on Tamiflu since this is the first day of your symptoms."

"Is there some kind of shot I can take? Will I get better in time for the wedding?" He was lucid enough to be worried about the ceremony.

"When is your wedding?"

"Saturday."

Dr. Thomas bunched his lips to one side and squinted his eyes in thought for a moment before nodding. "Yes, I think so. The medicine should shorten your illness by a few days. But give me a call if you're still not feeling well by Friday morning."

Madeleine walked him back to the car and took him to the pharmacy drive-through. Then she drove him home and walked him inside.

He decided the couch looked good and stopped there for a breather. He slid down until his head lay on the arm rest.

"You need to eat something before you take this." Madeleine stood beside him, reading the label of the pill bottle. "Have you eaten anything today?"

"No."

She was already walking into the kitchen. "I'll see what I can find."

There wasn't much in his fridge—he'd been trying to eat down his food supply since they'd be traveling soon. But Madeleine found an apple and some graham crackers.

"Here, can you sit up?"

He wasn't as helpless as Madeleine seemed to think, but being pampered was nice. Another perk to look forward to in married life.

Madeleine set up his TV tray by the couch and placed a plate with the apple—she'd even sliced it—and graham crackers on top. Beside that, she set a glass of water and his capsule.

"I like having you take care of me. You're very good at it. And so pretty. The prettiest nurse I ever had."

"You're feverish and you sound ridiculous." But she smiled and kissed him on the head. "Eat the food and take your pill."

While he munched on apple slices, she took his phone. "I'm setting an alarm for each dose so you don't forget." She set it on the couch when she finished. "Do you need to take another day off tomorrow?"

He shrugged. "I'll have to see how I feel."

Madeleine nodded, looking around the room. Clearly, she didn't feel comfortable leaving.

"Go." He waved his hand at her, flicking his wrist. "You have wedding stuff to do. I'm just going to take this pill and go back to sleep."

She grabbed her purse but still stood, watching him.

"Okay, see?" He placed the pill on his tongue and washed it down with water. "All gone." Then he stuck out his empty tongue to show her.

"I'll call tonight to check on you. Please get better soon." She backed away slowly.

"Bye. I love you."

"I love you too."

When the door finally closed, A.J. sighed and snuggled back onto the couch. He briefly wished Madeleine had grabbed a blanket for him before she left, but he couldn't find the strength to form the words. One last thought surfaced before he succumbed to sleep. Would Madeleine forgive him for ruining their wedding?

23

As much as Madeleine was worried about her wedding being completely derailed by the flu, she was more worried about A.J. She hadn't been prepared to see him so sick, and it wrecked her. She wished she could take his illness away or make him feel any better, but she was powerless.

The way he stumbled to the bathroom, it was obvious she'd have to help him walk if they were going to get anywhere in a reasonable amount of time. His weight on her shoulders almost made her trip, but she held up long enough to get to the car. When she made it back to the driver's side, she covertly rolled her neck back and forth.

His smile was dopey and his words were slurred when he talked, but A.J. with the flu was the most pathetic and adorable sight she'd ever seen.

Taking care of him felt like the most natural activity in the world for her to be doing. It killed her to have to watch him stagger back to the exam room without her. She'd have to have him add her to his emergency contacts as soon as possible. Then she'd also be able to go pick up his prescription for him while he slept at home.

When A.J. was all settled with his snack and his medicine, there was nothing else she could do. But she hated to leave him by himself. Worrying about him all day long wasn't helping anything. So she went shopping for chicken soup ingredients, saltine crackers, and ginger ale.

That night, she went back to check on him and to bring him dinner.

"A.J.? How are you feeling?"

The house was dark, and A.J. had apparently only moved to roll over on the couch and grab a blanket.

"Hey, Maddy." Although his voice was still groggy, he sounded more coherent than he had that morning. "I'm okay. How are you?"

Worried about you. The words hovered on her tongue, but she wouldn't let them out. He didn't need to add guilt to his long list of symptoms.

"Feeling better than you are, I'm sure." She walked past him to the kitchen, setting the soup and groceries on the counter. "I thought I'd bring you some dinner."

"Aw, that was sweet of you." A.J. sounded more lucid by the minute.

Madeleine returned to the living room and sat on the other side of the couch.

"Are you sure you should sit so close? I don't want you to get sick too." A.J. leaned away from her toward the end of the sofa.

"I've already carried you to the car twice. I think I'll be okay." But she relocated to the chair to make him feel better.

"Thank you for taking care of me today." A.J. tilted his head, gazing at her with compassion-filled eyes.

"It was my pleasure." Madeleine's heart squeezed as she looked back at him. "I'm not happy you're sick, but I am happy I got to be there for you today."

"Me too."

"I think you should take at least another day to rest."

Madeleine knew A.J. must be truly sick because he agreed right away to take a second day off. "I'll put in for a sub today. But I should go up to the building and print off tests."

"Those kids don't need your flu germs." In a school as small as Shady Springs, it wouldn't take much to knock out half the students with an illness. "Ask Aunt Clara to help you. She could print the test and sub plans in the morning before class starts."

"I don't know if I can spread flu germs on a piece of paper, but I'll accept the assistance."

"How about I help you send the email before I leave?"

All signs pointed to A.J. getting better, but she didn't trust him not to fall asleep straight away as soon as she left.

With A.J.'s help, she found his laptop and handed it over. While he was working, she ladled two bowls of soup and plated some saltine crackers.

"Do you think you can manage the walk to the dining room table?"

"You know, I did use the restroom today all by myself." A.J. scoffed from the sofa.

"I'm so proud of you." Madeleine's heart lifted to hear A.J. back to teasing and sarcasm. Little by little, the fear dissipated that he might not be fully recovered in time for the wedding.

They ate in companionable silence and Madeleine left after rinsing the dishes and storing the remaining soup in a plastic container.

Even if A.J. did get better in time for the wedding, she was going to be stuck taking care of last-minute preparations without him. Her mom was driving to Shady Springs tomorrow, and his parents were coming Thursday. They'd planned to have all of A.J.'s immediate family stay at his house, but maybe they should make other arrangements.

And what about all their other friends who were sick? Would they be missing bridesmaids and groomsmen because of this doomed vacation? *If only I hadn't let Shelby talk me into the trip, we wouldn't be in this situation.*

When she left for the night, A.J. was tucked in bed. For the millionth time that day, she prayed. *Please, Lord, let everyone heal quickly.*

Aunt Clara was waiting for her when she returned. "How's A.J. doing?" She looked up from the papers she was grading in the living room.

"Better. I think a day of rest—and some medication—helped a lot. Hopefully, after another day he'll be back to normal. Or at least healthy enough to stand at the altar."

"I got his email about sub plans. It won't be a problem to print those off tomorrow morning. And I'll make sure to check in on his sub."

"Thank you so much, Aunt Clara." Where would she be without her sweet aunt? Not about to marry the most handsome man in Shady Springs, that's for sure.

Clara wrote a number on the top of the test in her hand and piled it on a stack beside her chair. She glanced up at Madeleine. "Have you checked the weather lately?"

"No." A chill of foreboding settled in her gut. She didn't like the sound of Aunt Clara's question. "I've been too preoccupied. Is it supposed to get colder tomorrow?"

"Yes. And they're calling for a wintry mix on Friday and Saturday."

"What are the percentages?" Madeleine already had her phone out, checking her weather app.

Sure enough, a little image of rain and a snowflake sat below Friday and Saturday's dates on the app. Only a thirty percent chance though.

"Maybe it'll miss us."

"Yeah, nothing we can do about it anyway."

Aunt Clara was right, but the sentiment did nothing to ease Madeleine's nerves. Could anything else possibly go wrong?

24

———

$\mathcal{M}$adeleine groaned as she read the latest text from Jenna on Wednesday.

I tested positive for the flu.

Staci had already texted the same thing an hour earlier. She responded to both of them.

I'm so sorry! Get better soon.

She *needed* them to get better soon. How would she get through a wedding with no maid of honor and half her bridesmaids missing? Thankfully, Olivia and Felicity were still healthy and would be arriving Thursday with their parents.

What if it was an epidemic? What if even more people got sick? Oh, if only they hadn't all spent the weekend together, spreading germs around! Madeleine pushed those thoughts aside. There was absolutely nothing she could do about it. She'd taken all the precautions she could for herself. The rest was out of her control.

"When are we supposed to get the flowers?"

Madeleine looked up from her phone screen. Her parents sat across from her at Aunt Clara's kitchen table, her mom waiting for an answer to her question.

"Friday afternoon. I'll make sure we have room in the small refrigerator at church."

"You could leave them outside. It's cold enough." Dad smirked.

The temperature had dropped to just below freezing that week, and Arkansans were either grumpy about the colder weather or excited for the faint possibility of snow in December.

Nat King Cole singing on Aunt Clara's record player did little to soothe Madeleine's frazzled nerves. But the warm mug of coffee helped.

"It's only going to be cold, right? No chance of rain or snow?"

Madeleine waited while her parents both checked the weather on their phones.

"My app says only a twenty percent chance," Dad reported.

"Mine says twenty-five." Mom turned her phone off with a button and returned her focus to Madeleine. "We should probably make a plan, just in case."

"Just in case *what*?" Her voice rose in pitch. Madeleine took another sip of coffee.

Mom touched the tips of her fingers together in a steeple. "We might get some bad weather. Not snow, but maybe ice. What are we going to do if there's an ice storm?"

Tipping her mug back, Madeleine drained the last of her cup.

What was she supposed to say?

"I'm not canceling the wedding."

"No." Her mom shook her head vigorously. "No one is asking you to cancel. But could we delay the ceremony or restrict it to close family so elderly relatives don't feel pressure to drive in bad weather?"

Her heart squeezed, and her breathing quickened. She'd worked so hard. Surely all that planning and preparation wouldn't be for nothing.

She stood and crossed to the coffee pot. "Can we decide later? When we know for sure what's going to happen?"

Dad cleared his throat and swiveled in his seat. "Of course. We have no idea what's actually going to happen. No sense worrying about it."

As Madeleine opened the fridge to pull out some creamer, she caught Mom shooting Dad a wide-eyed glance. Madeleine pulled a spoon from the drawer of flatware and took steadying breaths as she swirled the creamer into her coffee.

"Didn't you have something you wanted to ask us?" Dad spoke calmly, shooting Mom a look of his own. He was clearly trying to help diffuse Madeleine's anxiety, but his question only served to increase it.

Madeleine had hinted to her parents that she had an important question to ask them. Although Aunt Clara and A.J. had both advised her to ask her parents about who should walk her down the aisle on Saturday, she'd avoided the subject for as long as possible.

If she didn't ask, then maybe whoever assumed they'd be walking her would show up, and she wouldn't be forced to have this difficult conversation. But, then, what if they both showed up? And what did she even really want?

"What is it, sweetie?" Mom smiled at her, waiting.

"I—" Nope. She couldn't do it. "I have some Christmas presents for you. Would you like them now or later?" She plopped down in her chair.

Mom's eyebrows shot up and her mouth formed an *O*.

"I assumed you had a question about the wedding." Dad laughed. "I keep forgetting it's Christmastime."

"I don't have your gift wrapped yet. How about we wait until after the honeymoon? Is that okay?"

"Sure, that's fine." Madeleine blew on her coffee before taking a drink. Back to Plan B—avoid the conversation and see what happened.

"What's on your to-do list for today?" Mom asked.

Madeleine nudged her notebook across the table, so both of her parents could see her scribbled list. "I want to get as much prepared as possible before tonight."

It was Wednesday, and there would be an evening devotional at the church building that night. But once the service was over at eight o'clock, Madeleine had free reign of the building. She'd asked her parents to come to Shady Springs that day to help.

"We still have to print programs, make signs, and string the ribbon on the wedding favors."

They made a plan to divide and conquer. Madeleine would hand letter chalkboard signs for the ceremony and reception. Dad had the most experience working with computers and graphic design, so he volunteered to print the programs. Mom claimed she didn't have enough artistic ability for anything except looping ribbon through the wedding favor ornaments.

Madeleine and her mom had gone back and forth over how much she was allowed to spend on wedding favors. Truthfully, Mom didn't want any favors at all. She'd complained that they were a waste of money and usually frivolous trinkets no one kept or remembered. Madeleine had talked her into a Christmas ornament she'd been able to order online at a discount. The front side had a copy of Madeleine's painting of a spray of flowers, part of the design from the invitations, and the back had Madeleine's and A.J.'s names with their wedding date and a Bible verse A.J. had selected.

Thirty minutes later, Madeleine had finished the first sign and took a break to check on her parents. Dad had a handle on the programs and had printed a few copies on Aunt Clara's printer.

"They look pretty good to me, what do you think?"

Picking up the paper, printed front and back with Madeleine's design, she briefly regretted not buying a heavier cardstock or having them printed professionally. But the budget only allowed for so much.

If half the bridal party is out sick, do the programs even matter?

"You're doing great, Dad." Madeleine grimaced. "But maybe we should print some without Jenna, Staci, Trey, and Brandon. Just in case they don't make it."

"Are you sure?" Dad's eyebrows raised, wrinkling his forehead.

"Yes." Madeleine nodded, handing the paper back to him. She may as well accept the possibility that her wedding might not go as planned. "Thank you." She gave him a quick hug before circling around to the dining room where her mom was stationed.

"I've got twenty done already. Once I figured out how long to cut the ribbon, it went a lot faster." She swept her hands over the neat piles laid out over the table. "I'm just nervous I'll run out of ribbon."

"I think I have another spool upstairs I can grab," Madeleine offered.

She jogged up to her bedroom, rifling through sacks and sacks of ribbon, lace, tulle, and other assorted decorative materials.

When she walked back to the dining room, Madeleine found her mom with a Bible in her hands.

"What're you reading?"

Strange for Mom to take a Bible study break in the middle of making wedding favors.

"I was just looking up the verse you put on the back of the ornaments." Her mouth was twisted to one side in a confused expression.

"It's that one from Song of Solomon, 'Set me as a seal upon your heart.'"

"I might have a different translation …" Mom handed over her Bible. "See?"

Madeleine picked up an ornament in one hand to check the reference. "Song of Solomon 6:8." She looked at the Bible in her other hand and her stomach dropped. "Oh no."

25

Mom bit her lip. "Do you think maybe it got mixed up?"

Placing the ornament on the table, Madeleine turned to Song of Solomon 8:6. She read, "Set me as a seal upon your heart, as a seal upon your arm, for love is strong as death."

Turning to Song of Solomon 6:8—the scripture referenced on one hundred beautiful Christmas ornaments on the dining room table—she read, "There are sixty queens and eighty concubines, and virgins without number."

Her breath caught in her throat and her eyes stung. What had she done?

"Mom." It almost came out as a moan. "What am I going to do?" She couldn't hand these out at her wedding. Since the verse wasn't written out, everyone would check the scripture on the back.

Mom stared back at her, wide-eyed and open-mouthed.

And then she laughed.

Madeleine watched as her mother clutched her chest and cackled until tears ran down her cheeks.

"What's wrong?" Dad burst through the dining room entryway. He looked at Madeleine and then at Mom.

Daughter and mother stood, one nearly crying from fear and mortification. The other crying from laughter.

Madeleine thrust the Bible in her dad's hands and ran up to her room.

Lifting a pillow from the bed, she smashed her face into it and screamed. She emptied her lungs until she couldn't yell any longer. Gasping for breath, she threw the pillow to the bed and flung herself over the covers.

God, why? Why is this wedding a complete disaster?

Was He trying to tell her something? If so, what?

Madeleine sobbed into the quilt on her bed, wailing as she released all of the tension and stress and fear she held in her chest.

When she'd finally quieted, she heard a light knock on the door.

"Come in," she whispered.

The knock sounded again.

"Come in," she croaked, a little louder.

Mom poked her head through the open doorway. "I'm so sorry for laughing, Maddy." Mom's eyes turned down at the corner, and tears threatened to release all over again as her mom swooped down to hug her.

She let out a sniffle, melting into her mother's embrace.

"I'm so sorry." Mom's voice was muffled against Madeleine's sweater.

"It's not your fault."

"I don't know what got into me." Mom pulled back to look into Madeleine's eyes.

Madeleine sighed. She straightened, sitting up on the bed.

"We're all so tightly wound right now. I think I might be going a little crazy."

"I know you weren't trying to hurt my feelings." Madeleine

pulled one leg up, shifting to a more comfortable position, and leaned against her mom. "It's all catching up with me. I keep working so hard to make this wedding great, and I'm met with disaster at every turn."

Mom wrapped an arm around Madeleine's shoulders.

"You've had just as many miracles along the way." Mom squeezed her in a hug. "Remember when you found the perfect bridesmaids' dresses at the thrift store? Or how we were able to get the invitations back before they were sent out? Or how you and A.J. found the perfect house in Sayers?"

Madeleine nodded, but she couldn't clear the dark clouds from her mind.

Why didn't she check the scripture? She'd spent so long designing those ornaments, fiddling with the layout until it was perfect.

How could she have missed the fact that she'd written a scripture reference for a Bible verse about concubines?

Madeleine brought her hands to her face.

Seriously? Could she have picked a worse Bible verse for a wedding favor?

She let out a giggle. "I guess I'm going crazy too."

Mom laughed. "Maybe."

"Let's hope our marriage includes just one wife and no concubines," Madeleine snorted.

"Yes," Mom said between laughs. "I don't know if King Solomon was the best example of marital faithfulness."

"I honestly don't know what to do." Madeleine sat straight again, slowing her breathing. "I don't think I can scratch out the wrong verse and correct it like we did with the invitations."

"Not even with a permanent marker?"

"The clear resin would make it look strange."

Mom nodded. "How about I help you with the signs and then we can figure out what to do?"

The rest of the day, Madeleine and her parents checked off

everything from the list, except the wedding favors. Every time she walked past the dining room, Madeleine grimaced and looked the other way.

Madeleine called A.J. later that afternoon.

"How are you feeling today?"

"Much better."

He sounded better too. Madeleine assumed the combination of medicine and rest had done the trick.

"Are you drinking plenty of water?"

"Yes, ma'am."

Madeleine could almost hear him roll his eyes.

"Okay, okay." She laughed. "I'm only trying to make sure you get better."

"I don't think my groomsmen have been so lucky."

Uh-oh.

"Trey and Brandon have already said they don't think they'll be able to come. I haven't checked yet with the other two."

Silently, Madeleine prayed everyone would recover quickly. "You know what? The only man I care about is you. As long as you're healthy, we'll be okay."

It was true. Even though anxiety twisted her stomach every time she thought about half their wedding party missing the wedding, the only person she actually needed was the man on the phone with her.

"Enough about me and the flu," A.J. said, interrupting her thoughts. "How was your day?"

"Dad printed both versions of the program, and I'm finishing up all the signs." Madeleine chose not to mention the wedding favors. He'd find out soon enough.

At dinner that night, Clara suggested they glue two ornaments back-to-back to hide the back.

"Or we could glue a bow over the Bible verse?" Dad winced as he said it, perhaps because he could tell it was a terrible idea.

"Or maybe we simply scrap the whole idea." Madeleine frowned, shoving a forkful of chicken in her mouth.

"I'm so sorry, sweetheart." Mom gave a sympathetic pout from across the table.

Madeleine finished chewing and wiped her mouth. "I just hate that I wasted all that time and money."

"Maybe no one will notice." Dad shrugged. He was clearly trying very hard to be helpful. They all were.

"Thank you, all of you, for your suggestions." Madeleine sighed. "Let's focus on what we *can* control. We've got a few hours tonight after church to decorate the auditorium. And A.J.'s family comes into town tomorrow. I'm going to make a list for the next two days."

Madeleine pushed her chair out from under the table and took her dishes to the sink.

She was getting married Saturday, no matter what. She just wished she could stop with the surprises already.

That night, the Shady Springs church building was a flurry of activity. Even though Madeleine had done her best to respectfully wait to start decorating until after Bible studies were wrapped up, curious churchgoers were eager to help out.

"How many tables are you wanting to set up in the fellowship hall?" Mr. Patterson asked, his arms folded over a Christmas sweater.

"Twelve," Madeleine answered. "Do you think we can fit that many?"

He sniffed and nodded, his lip protruding slightly. "We can sure try."

"And I'd like six long tables at the front for the food."

With several men busy moving tables and chairs, Madeleine turned her attention to the auditorium. Aunt Clara and Mom were pulling decorations out of the back storage room.

"I'd forgotten about these little pine trees." Aunt Clara

walked out, carrying two artificial trees attached to wooden boards at the bottom.

"And look at all this garland." Mom followed behind, arms laden with greenery.

"Madeleine?" A young woman spoke from behind her.

"Yes, hi, Sophie." Madeleine turned to see one of the high school girls from the youth group.

"I wanted to let you know we're moving all the props and decorations for the nativity play out of your way."

"Thank you," Madeleine said. "I appreciate you sharing your space with us."

Sophie smiled. "Of course. And we're planning to rehearse at my house this week, assuming the weather holds up."

Madeleine grimaced. She'd been trying not to think about the weather forecast. "I'm sure you'll be fine. Thank you."

By the end of the evening, the building looked worse than when they'd started. Garlands and lights sat in clusters on the floor. Boxes and bins of decorations lined the hallway. Stacks of round wood slices and candles waited on tables.

"By the end of tomorrow, this place is going to look great." Dad patted her back before walking with her out the door.

"I sure hope so. Because it's a mess right now."

26

The next morning, A.J. woke up feeling much more like himself. He still swayed a little when he stood up too quickly but was able to walk without too much trouble. And he was starving.

After a breakfast of dry cereal, he downed a dose of medicine and headed out the door. He still had two exams before the end of the semester.

Teachers at Shady Springs High School were given a limited number of sick days—A.J. figured they were supposed to save up all their illnesses for the summer. He didn't want to deplete every last day. Surely he was healthy enough to sit and watch kids take some midterms.

He dressed warm—in a sweater and slacks—but still needed his extra heavy jacket to make it to his truck comfortably. In the teachers' workroom, he waited in line to make copies of the exam.

"You got any big plans for Christmas break?" One of the older teachers in front of him asked. A light of recognition flashed behind her eyes. "Oh wait, you're getting married! Congratulations!"

"Thank you."

"Hope you don't get hit by this bad storm coming through." She grimaced.

A.J. hadn't paid any attention to the weather reports. He'd been too busy sleeping, trying to kick the flu before the wedding. "I hadn't heard about that. What are they saying?"

"Oh." She shrugged, clearly trying to backtrack. "Maybe ice or sleet. Maybe nothing."

Great. Did Madeleine know? He reached for his phone, but thought better of texting her. She had enough to worry about without him making it worse. Maybe it would turn out to be nothing.

He skipped the coffee pot—he'd always hated the taste—and filled up his jug of water instead.

A.J. stood in the hallway after the first bell rang and watched the teenagers stream down the hall from the cafeteria, where they waited in the mornings.

"Coach Young, welcome back!" One of his track students called to him.

He smiled and nodded, stepping back as his Arkansas History students trickled into the classroom.

"Okay, you know the drill. Make sure all your devices are turned off. If you're worried, hand me your phone and I'll keep it in a box until time is up." He walked around with a clear shoebox container, letting anyone who wanted to place phones in.

"You have an hour and a half. Keep the tests face down until I say … Go."

Now he waited. If he could stay awake the whole ninety minutes, he might be able to get some grading done.

But while he marked papers, periodically checking on students to make sure they weren't cheating, his mind wandered.

What was Maddy doing right now? Probably decorating the

church building and stressing out about centerpieces or something like that.

If he was being honest, he was glad to be at work and out of the storm of wedding preparations. Come this afternoon, his family would be in town to help get ready. He had another half day of work tomorrow—teacher in-service and lesson planning meetings—and then he'd be in the thick of it too.

His chest buzzed with excitement and nerves. Was he ready for the commitment? Their engagement had whizzed by in a frenzy. When he proposed to Madeleine, he'd been absolutely positive that he wanted to marry her, but he hadn't expected it to come so soon.

A.J. took a break from grading and stewing in his thoughts to walk around the classroom. He surreptitiously checked on students' progress. When he glanced at the clock, he was shocked to see only half an hour had passed.

Testing weeks were not his favorite.

Eventually, the last of A.J.'s students turned in her exam, and he could take a break from the quiet and stillness for a few minutes.

When he checked his phone, a missed call and text message from his mother flashed across the screen.

Headed your way. Be there around lunch time.

A.J. winced. He must've forgotten to tell his parents he'd be working today.

Quickly, he typed a message back.

I'm in class until 3, but I'm sure Maddy's up at the church building.

Hopefully they'd connect and not be waiting around at his house all day.

We can't get into the house without your key.
Should we stop by your office?

That was his dad. He couldn't seem to wrap his head around the fact that A.J. was a school teacher and didn't have an office.

No, check with Madeleine at the church
building. I'm giving tests right now.

He turned his phone off and stood to reset the classroom for the next group of students. They filed in gloomily. Everyone, himself included, would rather be at home in bed today.

They'd been quietly working on their exams for about thirty minutes, when A.J. spied a shadow at his door. A soft knock echoed through the stillness of the classroom.

As quickly as he could, without disturbing his students, A.J. tiptoed to the door.

"What is it?" he whispered.

A gangly kid of about fourteen stood in the hallway. He made no effort to lower his voice. "You have a call down at the office."

Why now? And who could it possibly be?

"I'm a little busy right now." A.J. widened his eyes, gesturing to the testers inside his classroom. "Tell them I'll call back later."

"They said it's an emergency."

A.J.'s heart raced. "Who was it?" What if Madeleine was hurt?

"I think it was your mom."

What if his parents had been in an accident?

"Can you watch my class?" The student took a step back, then looked to the left and the right as if there was another person to whom A.J. might've been speaking.

"Just for one minute." He tugged the boy inside and placed him in front of the whiteboard. A couple of his students glanced up and gave him curious glances, but they went back to work, scribbling furiously.

A.J. cracked open the door next to his and crooked his finger at Mrs. Miller. Once she was in the doorway, he whispered to her. "Could you watch my class for a minute? I have an emergency call in the office." Mrs. Miller nodded, and A.J. pulled the young boy out of his classroom.

The two of them took off down the hall, but A.J. easily outpaced him.

He burst in through the office door. "What is it? I have an urgent call?"

Ms. Bea nodded at him before handing him the receiver and pushing a button on her phone.

"Hello?"

"Oh, sweetheart, thank goodness you're okay." It was his mom.

"Mom? What's going on?"

"Well, we haven't been able to get a hold of you and we were worried."

What?

"Mom, I told you and Dad that I'm in the middle of midterm exams."

"But you didn't text me back."

A.J. bit his tongue to keep from screaming at her.

"I have to go. Please call Madeleine next time."

"Oh, I don't want to bother her."

But bothering *him* was perfectly fine?

Deep breaths.

"Mom, she'd be happy to talk to you. I'm sure she needs lots of help up at the church building right now."

That seemed to put Mom in a better mood. "Of course. We'll drive straight to the church building."

"Great. I'll call once I'm out of school. I'll see you soon."

"Love you!"

Ms. Bea raised an eyebrow. "Everything okay?"

Running his hands through his hair, A.J. sighed. "Yes, just an overbearing mother."

"We can all get that way sometimes." Bea smiled kindly. "Especially when our babies are getting married."

"I'd better get back to my class."

"Yes, you hurry on now."

A.J. allowed himself a quiet growl as he marched back down the hall. When would the madness cease? Could he make it through two more days? This wedding might possibly be his undoing.

27

If Madeleine didn't kill all of A.J.'s family before the wedding on Saturday, it would be a miracle.

> Please get here soon.

She texted A.J. for probably the tenth time in the last thirty minutes. It was already three-thirty. What was taking him so long?

"Do you like the bows bigger like this?" Ginger held up a massive sculpture of loops and tails made from ribbon and wire. "Or smaller, like this?" A medium-sized bow sat in Olivia's outstretched hands.

From the look on Ginger's face and the tone of voice she'd used, Madeleine could clearly tell she preferred the monstrous bow. But Olivia looked with disgust at both creations.

Madeleine had to agree with Olivia.

"I'm sorry, Ginger. I should've shown you the picture on my phone." Madeleine swiped through her photos until she came to the one she wanted. "Here."

It was a simple velvet bow—just two loops, not twenty—tied around a sprig of greenery.

"It looks pretty small." Ginger squinted at the phone screen.

"I was wanting to go with something more …" Tasteful? Aesthetically pleasing? "… Restrained."

Ginger twisted her lips in thought and nodded slowly. "That's one word for it."

"I'm not sure where you found this ribbon, but—"

"It was in the supplies your mom showed us." Olivia chimed in.

"Let me show you the ribbon I was hoping to use."

Once Ginger and Olivia were set up with the ribbon and the greenery, Madeleine went to check on her dad. He and Arthur were supposed to be hanging garland.

"A little higher on the right. No, too high."

Dad stood on the right side of the front stage holding an end of garland, while Arthur stood on the left side holding the other end of garland. And Mom stood several feet down the center aisle, directing them.

"Okay, now lower both sides," Mom called out. "No, too low."

"How's it going?" Madeleine stood beside her mom.

"Just great." Mom gave a falsely enthusiastic smile and thumbs up. Turning back to the front, she threw her hands in the air. "Ugh. Maybe we should start over."

Madeleine needed to leave the auditorium. If she stayed, she'd feed off of her mom's nervous energy and they'd both be absolute wrecks.

Walking back toward the foyer, she spotted Felicity slumped over in one of the pews. As Madeleine got closer, she could see that Felicity was on her phone.

"Want to help me with something?" she asked.

Felicity continued to stare at her screen, swiping occasionally.

"Hey, Felicity." Madeleine spoke a little louder that time. Nothing.

"Felicity."

Finally, she looked up. "What's up?"

"Want to help me with something?"

Felicity shrugged, but stood.

"Great. I'd like to get the tables and centerpieces set up and then work on the photo booth."

She led Felicity into the fellowship hall.

"First, we need to put on the tablecloths and then we can set out the round wood slices and candleholders."

Madeleine brought an armload of tablecloths from a closet. When she returned, Felicity was nowhere in sight. Poking her head around the corner, Madeleine found her staring at the mural of Jesus on the hall wall.

"You painted this?" Felicity's gaze ran back and forth over the painting.

"I did." Madeleine shifted the heavy load in her arms to be more comfortable.

They stood for a minute more. Madeleine almost didn't ask, but she sensed Felicity had something on her mind. "What do you think?"

"It's really good." Felicity reached out but stopped short of touching the wall. "It's hard to imagine you painted this when you still didn't believe."

Madeline redistributed the tablecloths in her arms to relieve some of the muscle strain.

"I became a believer *while* I painted it. Thanks to Sam's assignment to read the book of Matthew, and A.J. being so kind, and the other church members welcoming me."

As if only now seeing Madeleine, Felicity turned and reached out for her load. "Let me help you with those."

They divided up the tablecloths and got to work smoothing them over the round plastic tables.

"How did you know A.J. was right for you?"

Madeleine wondered at the suddenly serious Felicity. She'd never had a sibling, but she could tell something was going on with her. "It started as pure attraction." Madeleine shrugged. "I just thought he was really cute."

Felicity made a gagging noise.

"Hey, you asked!" Madeleine laughed. "But then, we had a lot of serious conversations and I realized I enjoyed talking to him ..." she wiggled her eyebrows. "... Every bit as much as I enjoyed looking at him."

"Ugh." Felicity rolled her eyes, but she smiled.

"Why do you ask?"

Felicity shrugged again. Madeleine wondered if that was all the girl knew how to do today.

A thought occurred to her. "Are you having boy problems?"

This time, when she shrugged, there was a shadow of a change with her. Something about the way her mouth turned up and her eyes widened.

"What's going on?"

Madeleine walked to a side table to grab some wood slices. She arranged three in a group on one of the tables while she waited for Felicity to talk.

"I had a guy I was talking to. I thought things were serious, but then he broke up with me right before Christmas break."

How could Madeleine care so much about a girl she'd only known a year? Her heart broke at the look on Felicity's face.

"I know it's probably silly." Felicity smiled, though her eyes sparkled with unshed tears.

"Can I give you a hug?"

When she didn't object, Madeleine wrapped her arms around her future sister-in-law.

"I'm so sorry."

Felicity squeezed back, for about two seconds, and then pulled away, swiping at her eyes. "It's just a little hard to watch you and A.J. be so happy and planning this beautiful wedding when I don't know if I'll ever find someone."

"You will." Madeleine wanted to hug her again, but sensed she'd reached her maximum touch allowance with Felicity. "I'm sure you will. And even if you don't, that's okay too."

"Thanks?" Felicity smirked, raising an eyebrow.

"I wasn't looking for a relationship when I found A.J., but I think God knew we needed each other." Madeleine took a moment to gather her thoughts, placing a pillar candle on one of the round wood slices on the table. "I think God will give you what you need when you need it. Does that make sense?"

"I think so." Felicity walked to the side table to grab some wood slices and imitated Madeleine's placement on the next table.

"I'm sorry if I'm not very good at this. You and Olivia are my only siblings." She bit her lip and gave a sheepish smile.

"Oh." Felicity swiveled her gaze to Madeleine. "I'd never thought of that before."

"I hadn't thought much about it either yet."

Maybe this was what having a bigger family was like. Sometimes you wanted to kill them and sometimes you wanted to hug them, but you always loved them.

But, seriously, when was A.J. going to show up?

28

The last block of A.J.'s day consisted of students needing makeup tests. While he waited for his students to finish, he was able to grade most of the multiple-choice questions but still had to read all of the essays his students had written. Plus, he had the tests from the last two days piled on his desk.

Just thinking about it made him tired.

A.J. checked the time. If he took a short nap, he'd be able to help Madeleine out without being so exhausted.

Slinging his backpack over his shoulder and grabbing the stacks of tests, he headed out the door. "See you tomorrow, Mrs. Miller. And thanks for your help earlier."

"Everything okay?"

"Yes, it was a false alarm. Everything's fine."

"Good. I'll see you tomorrow."

He gave a quick wave to the clumps of teachers talking in the hallway.

"Bet you can't wait for that wedding!" One of them called out.

"Sure can't!" He replied over his shoulder.

If he wasn't careful, A.J. could easily spend an hour of his afternoon chatting with the other teachers. But he was tired and everyone would assume he was preoccupied with wedding plans if he missed the afternoon gab session today.

The drive home seemed to stretch on and on, but he finally made it into his house, collapsing on his bed. He took a minute to burrow under the covers and was out in less than fifteen seconds.

* * *

Bang. Bang.

A.J. groaned, resurfacing from sleep.

"A.J.? We're coming in." His dad's muffled voice rang out.

He blinked and slowly turned toward his side. Reaching for his phone, he checked the time. Six in the evening. He'd completely missed helping out with wedding decorations at the church building. As well as dozens of text messages and phone calls.

I guess I forgot to turn my phone ringer back on after school.

Loud banging, stomping, and what was probably suitcase wheels sounded from down the hall. Voices, doors opening and closing. Then a quiet knock on his bedroom door. He sat up.

"Hi, sweetie. Madeleine lent us her key so we could get in the house." His mom stood in the doorway, her gentle voice reminding him of all the times she'd woken him in a similar way during his childhood.

"I'm sorry I slept so long and I never texted. I was exhausted after school today." Ironically, he'd probably have trouble sleeping tonight after that marathon afternoon nap.

"That's okay. You needed the rest." She perched on the corner of the bed. "We were going to find a restaurant for dinner. Do you want to come with us?"

"Yes." A.J. pulled both elbows back, stretching his chest. He stood slowly, thankful to not have another dizzy spell. "Let me wash my face and I'll join you."

After visiting the bathroom, he checked his phone again. Madeleine was clearly not happy with him.

Where are you?

I need help here!

Are you okay?

He dialed her number.

"A.J.?"

"Hey, Madeleine." He ran his fingers through his hair, pacing his bedroom floor.

"Where are you?" Her voice held tension and he could sense there were a lot more questions coming. "Are you okay? Why didn't you come to the church building after school?"

"I'm sorry. I was so beat after school, I came home to take a nap. I didn't realize how long I'd been asleep."

Madeleine sighed on the other end.

"I'm sorry," he repeated.

"I know you're still recovering and need your sleep. But you could've called or texted to let me know what was happening." Her voice wavered.

A.J. wished he could reach out and hug her. "I can still help tonight."

"It's too late. I mean, I'll still accept your help. But today was very stressful, and I could've used you there." She paused. "And I was worried about you."

"I'm sorry," he said for the third time.

"I know. You've already apologized." Big breath. "Just please text me next time."

"Okay."

Long pause. "Do you want to meet up for dinner? Dad called Mike's Diner and there's plenty of open tables for us."

"Sure. I'll let my family know."

So this is what it felt like to have your wife—or future wife—disappointed and angry with you. He'd certainly made Madeleine upset in the year they'd been dating. But he'd never felt the weight of responsibility like he did right now. She was depending on him and he let her down. He wasn't a single man anymore. Now he had someone else to worry about.

A.J. shared the information about Mike's Diner with his parents. While they weren't thrilled about the prospect of a greasy hamburger for supper, they agreed.

Walking into the restaurant, A.J. immediately spotted Madeleine. He wrapped her in a hug right away.

"I've been wanting to do that since we talked on the phone."

She didn't say anything, but he could feel her shoulders rise and fall with a deep inhale and exhale. Her arms squeezed around his waist.

One more breath and she pulled back. "Thank you. I needed that hug."

"Was today that rough?"

She grimaced as she nodded. "We made progress, but it was slow. I kept having to put out fires all day."

"Figurative fires?"

She laughed. "Yes, no literal fires. That's the last thing we need."

A mental image of a blockbuster-style fiery explosion flashed in his mind. He blinked quickly, banishing that thought.

Hand in hand, they walked to the counter. All around them, Madeleine's family and his family chatted. They sat at red and white tables, in plastic chairs or booths. Silver, green, and rainbow tinsel draped the front counter, the ceiling, and the front windows. Elvis's "Blue Christmas" played over the loudspeakers. With the chilly temperatures and dark sky, Mike's was especially warm and festive.

Even though Mom squinted and scoffed at the offerings on the menu, she eventually found a sandwich she could tolerate. Felicity and Olivia ordered milkshakes and fries and found themselves at a booth with Aunt Clara and Sam Sullivan, who'd been invited to join them.

Henry and Catherine stood, arms linked, laughing together over a private joke. They more than likely had lots of shared memories at this place. Madeleine had told him once that Henry worked here every summer he was home from college.

A.J. and Madeleine took seats at a little two-person table.

Looking around at the people in the diner, A.J. had a thought. He took Madeleine's hand.

"You know." He grinned at her. "We could get married right now."

"What?" Madeleine's smile slipped off her face. "What do you mean?"

"I could drive back to the house and grab our marriage license." He gestured to the booth next to them. "We have our preacher, we have our families."

"Are you crazy?"

"Yes." His grin spread wider. "Crazy for you."

Madeleine snatched her fingers away. "What in the world am I working so hard for if you just want to get married in Mike's Diner?"

"I never asked for a fancy wedding. I only want to marry you."

Madeleine smiled again, but the expression was clearly forced. "I want to marry you too. In a beautiful ceremony that honors our relationship."

A young woman walked up with their tray of burgers, fries, and shakes.

Settling in, A.J. decided to drop his suggestion. He'd never expected Madeleine to take it seriously. But as he chewed a fry, he watched his bride. She couldn't even jokingly consider a private ceremony. When did his sweet, kind, creative Madeleine turn into a ball of anxiety that even he couldn't unravel? Was this a preview of what was to come in their marriage?

29

Madeleine's eyes popped open the next morning. *It's Friday. Rehearsal day. Tomorrow is the wedding.* Her heart raced at the thought, and she slung her legs over the side of the bed. If it wasn't so cold outside, she'd go for a run to burn off all the nervous energy coursing through her body. Instead, she'd have to pour her efforts into composing a list.

Racing downstairs, she startled her aunt making coffee in the kitchen.

"I want to come up with an itemized schedule for each person for Saturday."

Aunt Clara raised her eyes over her mug. "Good morning to you too."

"And we need to call to confirm everything with the caterers and bakery. Do you think we have enough mints and almonds? Should we buy more? What about drinks? I should send Dad back to the store."

"I'd offer you coffee, but I think you're high strung enough already." Clara stood in place, observing Madeleine, taking occasional sips.

Madeleine ignored her aunt, skirting around her to reach for the coffee pot. "I'm fine. I just need a list."

"There's paper and pens in the junk drawer."

Madeleine knew this already. She'd spent the last year and a good portion of her childhood in Clara's home. But she thanked her aunt anyway.

Madeleine brought a cup of coffee, a pad of paper, and a pen to her usual seat at the kitchen table. Even though she hadn't asked for it, Aunt Clara poured a bowl of cereal and placed it before her. She absentmindedly scooped a spoonful into her mouth.

Time was slipping away, but the tasks kept piling up. How could she possibly finish everything before tomorrow?

She shouldn't only make a schedule for everyone for tomorrow, she should make one for today too. That way they could avoid the squabbles and misguided unhelpful "help" from yesterday.

While Madeleine scribbled away, Aunt Clara finished her coffee and began packing her bags. "I've got to head up to the school building. But I'll report for decorating duty as soon as our professional development is over."

"Do you think Sam will be available to help out again today?" Madeleine looked up from her paper.

"I don't know."

"It's just, you two seem pretty close. I thought you might know what his typical work schedule is."

"I think he usually works at the building on Fridays." Aunt Clara turned away quickly, zipping her bag, but Madeleine caught a hint of a blush on her cheeks.

She hadn't meant anything by her comment. Clara and Sam were very good friends. They spent a lot of time volunteering together with church activities.

Maybe there was more to that relationship than she'd realized.

Madeleine shook her head as a slow smile lifted the corner of her lips.

"We've got to pick up out-of-town guests from the airport, and I have to send someone to pick up A.J.'s ring today."

"Cutting it a little close, aren't you?" Clara hefted her purse on her shoulder.

"Yeah," she huffed. "I think we're going to be cutting it a little close on this whole affair." What had she been thinking when she decided to plan a wedding in less than three months?

She hadn't been thinking anything at all except that she wanted to marry A.J. Young as soon as possible.

* * *

A.J. had actually meant to work today. But as soon as his principal dismissed their last meeting, his coworkers hurried him out the door.

"You're getting married tomorrow."

"You have too much to do."

"Get out of here!"

After over four years of teaching with those men and women, he'd learned to listen to their advice. They promised to cover for him before sending him on his way.

A.J. showed up to a synchronized bustle of activity at the church building.

Friends and family members walked around, holding greenery or signs or strings of lights. In the center of it all was Madeleine, directing traffic and giving orders. He made his way through the people to stand in front of her.

Madeleine's shoulders dropped and a smile brightened her face. "You're here."

He took her in a hug. "I'm here."

Relaxing against him, her breaths slowed, her back expanding and shrinking with each inhale and exhale.

"What can I do?"

She pulled away to look into his eyes. "I hate to send you away, but I need you to pick up Matt and Shelby from the airport." She grimaced, her nose wrinkling in a very cute way. "And could you pick up the ring from the jewelry store? I hate to ask you to go get your own ring."

"Of course. I don't mind." He was happy to help diminish some of Maddy's stress. And, truthfully, he was relieved he would have a short reprieve from the noise and mayhem.

The flu medicine must be doing its job because A.J. hadn't needed to rest or blow his nose all morning. His head started getting a little fuzzy after the hour-long drive to the airport, but he had time to nap in the parking lot while he waited for Matt's text saying he'd landed.

A.J. pulled up to the arriving flights pickup zone to see Matt shouldering a backpack on his right and carrying a garment bag in his left hand. Shelby held onto a rolling suitcase and had a giant purse on her arm.

"Hi! Welcome to Northwest Arkansas," A.J. yelled through the open window of his truck.

"Happy day before your wedding!" Shelby called back to him.

Matt tossed his backpack and Shelby's suitcase in the bed of the truck. He hung the garment bag on a hook, and the purse went on the floorboard as Shelby and Matt squeezed in beside A.J. He wasn't always happy to have an older truck, but not having a console came in handy as they all squished in the front together.

They sped away from the airport and into Bentonville. A.J. always got a kick out of driving people to and from the XNA airport, surrounded as it was by farmland. Friends and family from bigger cities often thought he was going the wrong way because the airport was so isolated. That was Arkansas for you.

In his opinion, it was the best mix of metropolitan and country living.

"We need to stop by the jewelry store to pick up my ring real quick and then we'll head over to Shady Springs." He glanced at his friends. It was a tight fit with three grown adults in the front, but he figured being sandwiched next to Matt was less awkward than Shelby. Even if she probably smelled a lot better up close than Matt did.

"I'd ask how the wedding is coming along, but the fact that we're just now picking up your ring tells me everything I need to know." Matt laughed until a quick jab from Shelby and a yelp ended his laughter.

Every so often, A.J. glanced at his friends from the corner of his eye as he drove. Matt and Shelby were as entertaining as ever, even after years of marriage.

"Weddings are so stressful. I remember lots of last-minute crazy errands from when we got married too." Shelby glared at Matt briefly before turning a kind smile to A.J. "All that matters at the end of the day is that you're married."

"That's what I keep telling Madeleine, but she won't—or can't—listen to me." A.J. sighed, checking the mile markers for his exit. "It's like she's turned into a completely different person."

Shelby gave a sympathetic *hmm.* "She has it so much harder than you do right now. Try to support her as best you can."

"Yeah," Matt added. "She'll return to her normal self again after the wedding is over and the bridezilla alien parasite leaves her body."

"Gross, Matt." Shelby giggled, despite her admonishment.

"I'm just saying." Matt held up both of his hands. "This isn't forever. They all get like this."

"I'm sorry, 'they?'" Shelby made air quotes with her fingers. "You think I was a bridezilla?"

"Nooo." Matt dragged the word out, clutching Shelby by the shoulders playfully. His elbow bumped A.J.'s arm as he squeezed her. "Never, my dearest, the bride of my youth. You were perfect."

"I seem to remember a certain maid of honor getting a lecture on your big day," A.J. teased. He'd been a groomsman in their wedding, the summer after college graduation.

"That was my sister, and she deserved it. She was flirting with Matt's friends instead of helping me get dressed." Shelby wagged her finger. "And *then* she nearly missed her toast during the reception."

"Okay." A.J. laughed. "Fair enough."

"Just be patient with Madeleine," Shelby said, in a gentler tone. "She has a lot on her plate right now."

When A.J. pulled into the mall parking lot, they insisted on piling out of the truck with him and following him to the jewelry store. He tried on the ring, thankful to see it was a perfect fit, in more ways than one.

"Looks great on you, man." Matt clapped him on the back.

Shelby nodded. "It suits you. I like the style you chose."

On the way back to Shady Springs, Matt pointed to the dashboard. "It looks like you're running low on gas."

Glancing down, A.J. saw he was right. "We already passed the best place to get gas in Fayetteville. I have a place in Shady Springs on the way to my house that's pretty cheap. We can make it the rest of the way to the church just fine."

When they pulled into the church building parking lot, A.J.'s heart rate picked up. He was needed for wedding preparations. He knew he was. Secretly, though, he hoped Madeleine had errands for him to run the rest of the day. He wasn't sure how much more of this wedding he could handle.

30

That evening, Madeleine surveyed the auditorium. The gold curtains, which normally flanked the baptistry during services, had been pulled together, casting a warm glow. Tall candelabras lined the back of the stage, each draped with artificial greenery. Flocked evergreen trees at various heights stood just in front of the candles. The color scheme of shimmery gold, pine green, rustic brown, and winter white was coming together beautifully.

In her mind's eye, Madeleine could picture her bridesmaids wearing their burgundy dresses and standing in front of a crowd. They carried sprays of cedar, juniper, and white Star of Bethlehem flowers. She followed down the aisle, her ivory dress with its long lace sleeves and flowing skirt shining in the soft lighting.

Madeleine sighed. After all of their hard work, she was finally getting married. Despite everything—the flu, the catering fiasco, the terrible dresses, the changed dates, the ruined invitations (Did Uncle Lew ever get their phone messages?)— God had worked it all together to bring them here. She was still going to have an (almost) perfect wedding.

Blinking, she turned to look at the people who were actually surrounding her in the auditorium. Somehow, she and A.J. each had two bridesmaids and groomsmen who'd managed to stay healthy enough to come. Their immediate family, most of A.J.'s extended family, and a handful of ladies from the church had all come to the wedding rehearsal. To "help out."

Ginger and Arthur had opted to have soup and salad catered from The Sandwich Shop across the street for their dinner. Madeleine didn't mind the informal nature of the meal, and she was happy she'd convinced Ginger to use a large classroom in the older section of the building instead of the fellowship hall. She couldn't trust her friends and family not to spill soup all over her perfectly white tablecloths, ruining them for the reception tomorrow.

It was possible all these extra people were actually here for the food.

"Would you get everybody to the front, please?" Madeleine nudged A.J. It was time to get the show started. Several minutes past time, actually.

"Hey, everyone! Listen up!" A.J. called out over the crowd in his best teacher voice.

"I'd like the wedding party to come to the front of the auditorium. You're *all* welcome to stay, but please keep your voices down." A flurry of nerves tumbled through Madeleine's chest. She said a silent prayer that everything would progress smoothly. *All weekend long, God, please. Let it all go according to plan.*

"May I offer some advice?" Sam stood at her elbow.

"Of course." Madeleine was quickly realizing she hadn't thought through the proceedings of the wedding rehearsal.

"I'd suggest getting the wedding party up at the front the way you want them. We can practice the recessional and then the processional."

Start from the middle of the ceremony? Madeleine pinched

her lips together in thought. "I guess that can work. Should we practice the music at the same time?"

"Yes." Sam nodded. "We want everyone to get a feel for how slowly they should walk up and down the aisle."

Madeleine beckoned to Shelby. During the weekend in Branson, she'd asked her if she'd mind handling the music for the ceremony. "I've got my computer set up in the back. We're going to start with everyone up front, then we'll play the recessional music, and we'll walk back up the aisle with the processional music."

Shelby nodded and took her place by the laptop in the sound booth at the back.

"Let's go, people." A.J. clapped his hands, and Madeleine could imagine him on a field with a whistle. "If you're supposed to be up on stage, get there."

The wedding party took their places at the front. She half expected A.J. to congratulate his groomsmen on their "good hustle."

"Madeleine, you stand back and make sure everyone is where you want them," Sam encouraged her.

"A.J. move to the right a bit," Madeleine called out. "Wait, no, your left … a bit more."

After a few minutes, each person was perfectly situated. Madeleine breathed a contented sigh. "Perfect." She made her way to A.J.'s side.

"Wait!" Olivia stopped her, stepping away from her place on stage.

Madeleine froze in place.

"You can't come up here." Olivia waved her hands. "It's bad luck."

"We don't believe in luck, Livvy." A.J. scoffed, head tilted toward his sister. He gestured to Madeleine. "Come on up, it's fine."

She hesitated. "I don't know. We'd better not risk it."

"Seriously? Don't be ridiculous." A.J. propped his fists on his hips.

Madeleine looked at Sam. She'd trust his authority on this question.

"You do whatever you want, Madeleine."

She bit her lip. "I'll have Aunt Clara stand in for me, if that's okay." She gave A.J. a pleading look. "This way I can watch and make sure everything goes well."

A.J. rolled his eyes, but he didn't say anything more.

Aunt Clara hurried up on stage, winking down to Madeleine, and Sam talked through an abbreviated version of the ceremony. Madeleine couldn't help but notice the way he tenderly gazed at Clara and his voice grew husky as he recited the vows.

Of course, A.J. did not repeat any vows to Madeleine's aunt —and Clara didn't say anything at all during the rehearsal—but Madeleine wondered if she wouldn't be witnessing Aunt Clara's wedding in the near future. The thought warmed her heart.

With only a slight hiccup, Shelby played the recessional music and the bridesmaids walked down the aisle with the groomsmen.

"Should we run through the ceremony from the top now?" Madeleine called up to Sam. He was doing a much better job of directing the rehearsal than she'd have done on her own.

"Yes," he called back.

Madeleine held up a finger to Sam and sprinted out to the foyer to grab two programs. She handed one to Shelby. "Here's the order we'll go in." Madeleine clicked a button on the laptop. "There's the music for the prelude while everyone's getting seated. We'll have the grandparents and family come in on this song." She guided Shelby through the program briefly, then walked up the aisle to hand a program to Sam.

"Should we practice lighting the candles?" Mom asked from her seat.

"That's a good idea. Who do we have lighting the candles?"

Had they picked someone for the job? Was that another detail she'd let slip?

Ginger spoke up. "I believe the families light the candles. That is, if we're using a unity candle later in the ceremony."

She hadn't thought about a unity candle.

After a quick pause while Dad ran to find two lighters and an extra candle, Mom and Ginger each lit one candle on the end with a lighter, then used those candles to light the rest. The effect was stunning. Tiny flames flickered and danced, candelabras gleamed, and Madeleine got the feeling she was in a winter wonderland.

Dad lowered the dimmer switch at the back, giving just enough light to see but not enough to distract from the glow of the white Christmas lights and candles.

Shelby hit the button for the next track, and the grandparents and parents walked up the aisle to their seats.

Next, Felicity and Olivia each took their turn walking to the front. Madeleine had accounted for twice as many bridesmaids, so there was a portion at the end of the song with nothing happening, but perhaps it would add to the dramatic suspense.

Then Madeleine realized something else she'd forgotten.

Her dad stood by her side, expectantly. Her mom stood nearby.

They had never talked about who was going to walk her down the aisle.

Icy dread spread over her chests. What should she do?

"Fire!"

Torn from her internal dilemma, Madeleine's brain took a beat to catch up to her eyes.

At the front of the auditorium, her beautiful winter wonderland was quickly burning to the ground.

"Fire!"

Fire!

A.J.'s body began moving before his mind caught up. He'd long ago learned where all the fire extinguishers were throughout the building. In fact, he'd had to go through different training courses on fire safety and first aid for their insurance company.

Some unused corner of his mind knew to open the door to the side of the stage. There was a tiny hall connecting to a changing room and stairs leading up to the baptistry, and there was a door to the outside. But A.J. ignored both of those to rip the bright red fire extinguisher from the wall.

From the corner of his peripheral vision, A.J. could see Sam going through the same motions, a few beats behind, on the other side of the auditorium, where there was a second fire extinguisher.

A.J. had never used a fire extinguisher before. He'd only watched videos of someone else doing it. But the concept seemed simple enough.

He found the silver ring at the top of the device and yanked.

The fire was quickly spreading, trailing along the greenery, inching closer to the pine trees below.

Bridesmaids and groomsmen had cleared off the stage and stood somewhere behind him. He heard confused, muffled yelling.

A.J. took the nozzle in his right hand, aimed at the base of the flames on the closest candelabra, and squeezed the trigger.

Yellow dust shot out of the nozzle. He sprayed the powder in an arc over the entire right side of the stage while Sam did the same on the left. Even when he couldn't see a flame anymore, he held down the trigger. When the device only spit out dusty sputters, he lowered his arm.

The adrenaline coursing through his body slowed, so he could see clearly the scene before him.

If Madeleine had wanted a winter wonderland, A.J. and Sam had delivered.

The entire stage was blanketed in powder. The spindly shapes of candelabras and triangles of trees were now a light yellow. A cloud of yellow ballooned from where the fire once was. A.J. turned into his elbow to cough.

Turning to find Madeleine, A.J. heaved a sigh of relief. As far as he could tell, no one was injured. And the church building hadn't burned down.

But Madeleine's face told a different story.

* * *

Madeleine couldn't believe it.

She stood rooted to the ground, her mouth hanging open. Wide eyed, she took in the scene around her. Similarly, gaping mouths and shocked faces surrounded her.

The beautiful decorations they'd all worked so hard on the last three days were completely ruined.

All those hours of labor, all the money she'd spent on

182

supplies to fill in the gaps of what the church provided, all of it was wasted.

A.J. stood in the middle of it all, an almost pleased look on his face.

She had no words.

A red, hot anger boiled up inside of her.

She could blame their moms for being careless. She could blame whoever hung the greenery too close to the candles. She could blame A.J., although she knew he'd saved them from an even bigger disaster.

Why, God? Why did this have to happen?

Madeleine brought her hands to her face, rubbing her eyes, and bringing her fingers to pull at the roots of her hair. The motion did little to calm her.

"Are you okay?" Mom wrapped an arm around Madeleine. She called out louder to the rest of the auditorium. "Is everyone okay?"

She gave Madeleine a squeeze and then moved on to the older relatives, escorting them out to another room. Madeleine assumed it was to avoid the powdery dust settling over everything.

A.J. walked off the stage and toward her. "I'm so sorry I ruined the decorations." His expression, which had been relieved and pleased only moments before, showed tenderness and sympathy.

She should be grateful everyone made it through the fire unscathed. She should be thanking A.J. and Sam for stopping the fire. But she couldn't push back the flames in her belly long enough to feel anything else.

"We need to get this cleaned up." Aunt Clara, ever the practical thinker, marched up to the stage and surveyed the damage, hands on her hips. "I'll go get a vacuum cleaner."

"I think we have a second one in my office." Sam set down the fire extinguisher and jogged off in that direction.

"Madeleine, A.J., how about you grab some trash bags?" Clara asked before opening the same side door Sam had gone through to find the fire extinguisher. She disappeared a moment before lugging out an industrial sized vacuum cleaner.

While she plugged the machine to the wall, A.J. took Madeleine by the hand. "There are some trash bags in the kitchen."

They walked past family and friends, all of whom still looked rattled, to the foyer.

"It's going to be okay, Madeleine. We'll figure this out."

How? How could they possibly salvage this wedding?

32

After about thirty minutes of vacuuming, bagging trash, and wiping down surfaces, there wasn't too much yellow powder left. There also wasn't much left of Madeleine's design.

One of the trees had melted beyond repair and needed to be tossed. The candelabra that caught fire had turned a tarnished black instead of silver. All of the tulle covering the stage—which had previously been disguising the bright blue carpet—was permanently yellow.

What was the point?

The longer Madeleine stared at the scene before her, the more hopeless she became.

"The caterers are here," Ginger announced. "Let's all wash up really well and grab some food."

Madeleine didn't move from her spot. She figured she should wait for her guests to go through the line first. The sound in the auditorium lessened at a decrescendo until the last guest walked through the wooden double doors.

A.J. moved to stand beside her. They stood together, facing the stage. "It doesn't look too bad," he said.

"How can you say that?" Her anger, simmering below the surface all evening, boiled over. "Our wedding is ruined!"

"No, it isn't." A.J. rubbed her arm softly.

The sensation irritated her, causing her to shiver, and she slapped his hand away. Goosebumps covered her arms. Not from a pleasant tingly feeling, but from a heightened buzzing fury.

"Don't you care about any of this?" Madeleine knew she should keep her voice lower, but only A.J. could hear her now. The rest of the guests were lining up for soup and sandwiches down the hall. They wouldn't hear unless she screamed at the top of her lungs. Although the thought was tempting.

"Of course I care."

"Then why am I the only one doing everything? Why do you act like this is all no big deal?" She swept her hands, gesturing to the front of the room, where all of the damaged decorations hung limply, still dusty and faded from their harrowing ordeal.

"What are you talking about? I've been working my tail off too. And for what?" A.J.'s voice grew in volume. Pink splotches crept up his neck.

Madeleine didn't remember ever seeing that happen before. Maybe she'd never truly made him angry.

He slashed his hand through the air. "You act like the only thing that matters to you is this wedding."

"Yes." Madeleine nearly laughed at how ridiculous he sounded. "It *is* the only thing that matters right now."

The splotches were darkening, growing redder with each minute they kept yelling at each other. "What about our marriage?"

Madeleine stepped back. "This wedding *is* our marriage. There is no marriage without a wedding."

Taking a deep breath, A.J. tugged his fingers through his hair. "No. We could sign the papers today and be married. We don't need this." He waved his hands around wildly. "Any of this."

"So you want to just throw away our wedding? Isn't our relationship worth a ceremony?" She shook her head and rocked back on her heels. "Don't you want to honor our marriage with something special?"

"Of course, I do." A.J.'s voice came out in a bark. He filled his lungs with air and spoke again, softer now, but still laced with tension. "Of course, I do."

A.J. reached out for her hands, but she pulled away.

"Then why are you acting like none of this matters?"

"Because it doesn't!" All signs of the temporarily cool and calm A.J. were gone. His breaths were shorter and louder. "None of this is important in the long run."

She couldn't look at him.

Her blood boiled a bright scarlet. Her pulse raced.

"Seriously?"

She'd finally lost all control.

"Maddy? Is everything okay?" Dad poked his head through the back doors of the auditorium.

She gulped in a breath. "No."

Pushing off the pew she stood beside, Madeleine marched to the back of the auditorium and through the foyer. With a forceful shove, she pushed open the glass doors that led to the parking lot. She found her car where she'd parked it that morning and flung open the door.

If none of this mattered to A.J. then what was the point?

She'd let him deal with the clean-up and decorations. She'd spent enough time and energy on this wedding. Every last detail had been hand-designed and selected by her. And for what? Her own groom didn't even care. None of it mattered to him.

Fuming, she peeled out of the parking lot and away from the church building.

* * *

A.J. took labored, heavy breaths after Madeleine stormed out of the room. Even after she'd been gone a while, he struggled to get his blood pressure under control. Why did this woman have such control over him?

Because you love her.

Ugh.

He kicked the wooden pew beside him and immediately regretted it, his toe pulsing from the self-inflicted wound.

If he wasn't so furious at her, he'd chase after Maddy and beg her to come back. But she'd want an apology and he wasn't ready to give one.

He knew he was right.

She'd been hyperfocused on this wedding for the last three months, stuck in tunnel vision. And nothing A.J. said or did helped. He couldn't perform any of the tasks she'd taken on. He was inept at anything creative or artistic. She didn't want to listen to reason. She'd barely taken an interest in their pre-marital counseling, although she had at least completed her homework for the last few sessions.

A.J. growled in frustration.

"Um, do you think she'll be okay?" Henry still stood in the back of the auditorium.

"I don't know." He couldn't say he didn't care, but he sure didn't understand this version of Madeleine. And he wasn't about to pretend he could predict what she'd do next.

"What happened? I heard yelling." Catherine joined Henry in the doorway.

"We got into an argument." A.J. rubbed his hand on the back of his neck. "We can't seem to see eye-to-eye on the importance of wedding decorations."

"Ah." Catherine nodded slowly.

"I guess you'll say I should go after her."

Catherine twisted her lips in a thoughtful expression. "No, I don't think so."

"Why not?"

"She needs time to cool off. I bet she'll be apologizing to you before too long."

Henry nodded knowingly. "She was like this as a kid too. When she gets angry—really angry—it's best to give her a few minutes."

Was this a red flag? Should he be concerned about the future of his marriage?

Catherine held up a hand. "I haven't seen her get truly angry in a long time. I think she's mostly grown out of her bad temper."

"No, and she never even tried to run away as a little girl." Henry looked at Catherine. "Unless she did when I was out of the picture."

"No." Catherine grabbed his hand and gave a soft smile. "No, she never did. Usually, she'd go to her room and be fine in a few minutes. Here." She held up a finger. "I'll check my phone."

Catherine opened her location app and found the little dot that indicated Madeleine.

"There she is, back at Clara's house." She turned off the screen and returned the phone to her pocket.

With the matter settled, all three of them looked around the auditorium. The ends of the pews still held the bows and sprigs of evergreen Madeleine had attached. Some of the decorations up front were untouched. But most of it was unusable. And the effect of the scene was depressing, made even worse by the fact that he knew how much work had gone into its creation.

"Amazing how it only took a few seconds to ruin three days' work." A.J. stuck his hands in his pockets.

Henry frowned. "How are we going to fix it?"

"Hmm." Catherine twisted her lips and squinted at the stage. "I have some ideas. But we need help, and you need some food." Smiling, she took his arm. "It's going to be okay, A.J."

He prayed she was right. He'd need more than okay if he was ever going to please his ill-tempered bride.

As it turned out, Catherine wasn't the only one with ideas. A.J. had only to ask, and his friends and family began talking over each other with all of their grand plans to restore the church auditorium to its previous beauty.

"Don't they sell some of those electric candles at the store?" Mom asked. She and Dad volunteered to make a run to the grocery store and the hardware store around the corner to look for supplies.

"I can't believe Madeleine paid money for all these tree branches," his aunt said. "I bet we could find a million by walking around town." A troop of cousins took off in search of evergreen boughs.

"Sam, could we borrow some of the poinsettias from your front porch?" Clara asked. "And I can bring some of mine from home." The two of them left to gather Christmas decorations to borrow for the wedding ceremony.

Everyone contributed thoughts and ideas, and before long, each person had a job to do.

With all of the family and friends pitching in, there was more than a little confusion. But, somehow, in only two hours, they were able to throw together something halfway decent.

Sure, the color scheme was a little less … unified … than Madeleine's original design, but it worked. On either side of the stage, poinsettias borrowed from Sam's and Clara's houses stood in front of urns filled with pine tree branches. Fluffy fake snow —borrowed from Clara's Christmas house collection— cushioned the urns and softened their appearance. Electric candles replaced the real ones from before. And evergreen boughs adorned the cleaned and polished candelabras, attached with zip ties from the teacher resource room.

"What do you think?" A.J. asked Catherine. As Madeleine's mom, he figured her approval was the best indicator of what Madeline would say when she saw their attempts at decorating.

"It turned out nicely," Catherine said with a hesitant smile. "All things considered."

"Oh, we pulled off quite a feat." Clara laughed, brushing off her hands. "And now we should all get some sleep for tomorrow."

"I think we need to salt the driveways." Sam spoke in a low volume, so only A.J. could hear him. "I didn't want to say anything to make the situation more tense. But we're supposed to get some bad weather tonight."

A.J. nodded. "I've heard that too. Do we need to buy some salt?" The hardware store was closed at this time of night, but they could drive to Fayetteville.

"No," Sam said. "I picked some up yesterday when I saw the forecast."

With the help of Henry, Cole, Matt, and his dad, each entrance and exit got a thorough application of ice melting sodium chloride.

"Don't want to put this stuff on my French fries, but it should help keep the ice from freezing." Henry sprinkled the last of a bag on the sidewalk leading to the kitchen door.

"How bad do you think it'll be?" A.J. asked.

"We can't know for sure, but the weatherman said to expect a wintry mix all night long." Sam reached out his hands for Henry's empty bag, stuffing it into a trash sack.

"Don't worry, man. It'll be fine." Matt gave a smile that should've been reassuring, but A.J. wasn't convinced. Not after everything else that had happened.

* * *

Madeleine couldn't sleep.

She'd left in such a rage, she hadn't stopped to really think about what she was doing. Once she'd driven back to Aunt Clara's house, her pulse had slowed. And by the time she'd washed her face and dressed for bed, she was more hungry than anything.

After tossing and turning, adjusting her pillows, and pulling her sheets up to her chin, Madeleine gave up on trying to go to bed early.

I really should've grabbed a sandwich before I stormed off.

She pulled on a robe and padded down to the kitchen in search of sustenance. She knew by heart which steps creaked the loudest after living with her aunt for over a year. But there was no need to be so quiet. On reaching the first floor and poking around, she discovered she was alone in the house.

The others must still be enjoying dinner at the church building.

She opened the fridge, searching for leftovers. A tub of butternut squash soup. Pasta from last week that should probably be thrown out. Roasted chicken with veggies.

Madeleine pulled the soup out of the fridge and placed it in the microwave.

While she waited for her food to heat, she stuck two pieces of bread in the toaster and grabbed a spoon and a glass of water.

When the timer dinged, she gingerly carried the tub to the kitchen table. *No point in getting a bowl dirty.* She set it straight on a placemat.

At first, while she sat at the table alone, munching on toast and sipping her soup, Madeleine thought of absolutely nothing. Her anger and hunger had cleared her head of any other thoughts. Now that she was home alone and eating food, there was nothing left.

She sipped on her water, washing down a bite of toast.

Her perfect wedding was never going to happen.

Madeleine stared down at her dinner. Crumbs from her toast dusted the placemat.

After all her hard work, after years and years of dreaming about the day she said "I do," Madeleine was going to have a shoddy, thrown-together, slapdash wedding. They didn't even have a full wedding party. All she really had was a dress, a photographer, and a groom. Except now her groom was probably furious with her.

If she didn't have soup right in front of her, Madeleine would've thrown her head down on the table. Instead, she spooned another mouthful.

What was the point? She didn't have enough energy for dramatics anymore.

Madeleine slumped in her chair and sighed.

God, I tried so hard. I worked so hard on this wedding. And for what?

What had it all been for?

She'd told herself and A.J. it had been for their marriage. A perfectly organized, decorated, and coordinated wedding would honor their union and set them up for success. So what about the ceremony she was about to have tomorrow? What kind of marriage would that signify?

Maybe this is the most honest version. I was only pretending to have my life together, anyway.

Perhaps a chaotic wedding was the most true-to-life representation of her relationship with A.J.

Madeleine drained the last of her soup and carried her dishes to the sink. She rinsed everything and set it all in the dishwasher.

Walking back to the living room, Madeleine remembered the conversation she'd had with Aunt Clara and Nancy Jones when they were addressing wedding invitations. Back when she'd thought everything was going well.

Among Clara's many photographs on the wall, the pictures from Aunt Clara and Uncle George's wedding were some of her favorites. Everyone looked so happy. Madeleine gazed at the happy family captured in the pictures.

Aunt Clara had said the cake was dry and the music was off-key. But she radiated joy because she only had eyes for Uncle George.

She turned away from the wedding photos to climb the stairs. Each step took effort, as though her legs were made of lead. When she reached her bedroom and pushed open the door, her gaze landed on the bridesmaids' dresses hung on the hook on her closet.

What had that woman at the thrift store said? She remembered being so irritated at the time, but the prayer was more appropriate than she'd realized.

She'd said that the marriage itself is the important part. And that the wedding was nothing compared to the life she and A.J. would live together.

A.J. was right. She'd been focused on all the wrong things.

Swallowing past the lump in her throat Madeleine reached for her phone. She didn't trust herself to call him right now. Her emotions were still too raw. She wasn't angry at him anymore, but she was still broken-hearted over the state of her decorations.

She typed out a text message, deleted it, and typed again.

I'm sorry. I love you. Please forgive me. You were right.

Hopefully that captured everything she needed to say and he'd understand her loud and clear.

Madeleine checked her phone again before retiring to bed. Voices filtered up the stairs, so she knew her parents were back at the house, but she still had no answer from A.J.

She prayed he'd still want to get married tomorrow.

34

The next morning, the town of Shady Springs woke to a glittery world of ice. Madeleine opened her blinds to see icicles covering the bare tree branches outside her window. Ice crystals had formed on the glass and sparkling frozen particles covered the ground below.

The ice storm had come while she was sleeping.

Lord, please let this be the last catastrophe to fall upon this wedding.

She bundled up in her robe before heading downstairs.

"Good morning, sweetheart. Happy wedding day." Mom held out her arms and Madeleine let herself fall into her mother's embrace.

She'd slept fitfully all night long and wanted to cry on her mother's shoulder, but she held herself together. After one last squeeze, she let go and made her way over to the coffee pot.

"I don't know about you two, but the storm last night kept me awake. I kept hearing popping and creaking. It made me so nervous." Clara shook her head as she stirred sugar into her mug.

"Have you checked for storm damage?" Mom asked.

"As far as I can tell, I only had a few smaller branches fall."

Clara took a sip of her coffee. "I'll have to check the roof, but I think we escaped without any major damage."

"What about the rest of the town?" Mom pulled a stack of plates from the cabinet.

"I don't know." Clara frowned. "We can check the news or social media, but we'll have to wait and see."

Footsteps sounded on the stairs and in the hallway before Dad walked through the kitchen doorway. "Good morning, everyone."

He walked over to give Mom a kiss—something that still threw Madeleine off—before grabbing a mug of coffee for himself.

"Good thing I made a big pot this morning." Clara raised the mug in her hand. "I think we're going to drink every last drop."

"I'm glad you didn't lose power last night." Dad wrapped his hands around his cup.

Madeleine hadn't considered all the possible ramifications of the ice storm. What if the church building had no power? And what about all the guests staying at hotels in Fayetteville? Would they be able to make the drive to Shady Springs?

Anxiety fizzed inside her chest. She could feel her blood pressure rising, and she took a slow, deep breath.

It would all be okay. It had to be.

She grabbed a banana and a cinnamon muffin from the counter before joining her mother at the table.

"Let's finish breakfast and load up the cars quickly. I want to get over to the church building fast so we can assess the situation." Madeleine spoke in clipped tones, attempting to sound like she had everything under control, but she feared she sounded harsh and controlling.

"Sure thing, sweetie." Mom patted her hand.

Clearing her throat, Aunt Clara looked pointedly at Mom and Dad, gesturing with her head to Madeleine.

Subtlety was never Clara's strong suit.

"What is it?" Obviously, they'd talked about her last night, but Madeleine wasn't sure what kind of lecture she was in for this morning.

"We wanted to check and make sure everything's okay." Mom rubbed her back.

"Of course, all weddings are stressful and that's normal," Dad chimed in. "But ..." He grimaced, trailing off.

"You just seem to be having a hard time." Mom finished.

"What? Because I shouted at A.J. and ran out of the church building in the middle of the rehearsal dinner?" Madeleine attempted to keep a straight face.

"That about sums it up." Clara laughed from her spot leaning against the kitchen counter.

Madeleine chewed a bite of her banana, then took a drink of water. "I texted A.J. last night, but I should apologize to you as well." She gazed around the kitchen at the three pairs of eyes staring back at her. "I'm sorry. Planning a wedding in such a short amount of time was even harder than I thought it would be."

Mom nodded but didn't say *I told you so*, even though she could truthfully say she'd warned Madeleine many times.

"It would be hard for anyone." Clara walked to the table, concern etched on the features of her face.

"I know, and I really worked to make this the perfect wedding, but I don't think it's going to happen."

Madeleine thought her parents and aunt might say something along the lines of *Oh, don't worry, it* will *be perfect.* Or maybe *Your wedding will be great, just wait and see.*

But instead, Clara laughed again, and her mom said, "That's impossible."

"As a photographer, I've been to a lot of weddings." Dad slid into the chair across from her. "Wanna guess the one thing they all had in common?"

"They all got married at the end of the day?" Madeleine ventured.

"No." Dad raised his eyebrows. "Actually, there was that one …" He turned to Mom. "Remember?"

"Oh yeah!" Her eyes widened, then turned suddenly somber. "That was sad."

"Okay, so what was it?" Madeleine asked before they could launch into a tangential side story.

"They all had something go wrong," Dad said before taking a sip of his coffee. "Every single one."

"But did they have every last aspect of the wedding go terribly wrong? Because I might have them beat."

"You might," Dad agreed, pouting in a sympathetic expression. "You've had a rough time of it, Maddy."

"But you'll make it even harder on yourself if you keep expecting everything to be perfect." Clara brought over the tray of muffins.

Mom leveled her gaze at Madeleine. "Trust me, as someone who struggles with perfectionism, striving for a perfect wedding is a losing battle. You're only going to be disappointed."

"I think I'm starting to see that." Madeleine pinched a chunk off her muffin before popping it in her mouth. The cinnamon and sugar reminded her of Christmases past with Aunt Clara and her parents. The problems of the world shrank down to a manageable size with the three of them by her side.

"But I still really wanted a nice wedding. Is that so wrong?"

"Of *course* not," Mom said emphatically. "But let's keep the most important things most important."

Her mouth was full, so Madeleine simply tilted her head in confusion.

"Mom means that your marriage with A.J. is more important than the decorations, the cake, or even—" he pointed to himself "—the photographer."

"Right. You're starting off on the right foot because you're both trusting in God and committing to love Him first." Mom nodded. "Not because of how nice everything will be at your ceremony."

"You can have a beautiful wedding and a terrible marriage." Clara pursed her lips knowingly.

"And you can have a beautiful marriage and a terrible wedding," Dad said, quickly interjecting, "Not that I'm saying your wedding will be terrible."

"Sure, Dad." Madeleine laughed.

She was amazed she could laugh about that now.

Mom checked the clock on the microwave. "Let's say a prayer for this breakfast we've eaten and for Madeleine and A.J. We've got to get to the church building, perfect wedding or not."

Dad reached out for Madeleine's hand, Mom took her other hand, and Clara scooted closer to wrap her arm around her shoulders. Madeleine felt wholly and completely loved by her family and by God in that moment. She squeezed her eyes, soaking in Dad's words and the feeling of the Holy Spirit's presence in the room.

Lord, I pray I won't forget to love you first. And please let us all get to this wedding safely.

35

When they'd finished eating breakfast and gathering items for the wedding, Madeleine, her parents, and her aunt piled into Mom's car. Of all four vehicles at the house, Mom's was the most likely to survive the trip over icy roads to the building.

In warmer weather, Madeleine had walked from the church to Aunt Clara's house. Today the drive would take quite a bit longer than usual.

Mom drove her car at a snail's pace, clutching the steering wheel. She was used to driving in snowy weather—Kansas City usually got a decent amount of snow, and she'd grown up in Wichita, Kansas. But an ice storm on the day of her daughter's wedding seemed to be giving her anxiety.

A chiming came from Madeleine's pocket. She pulled out her cell phone and checked the screen. It was the caterers. Icy dread snaked through her.

"Hello?"

"Hi, is this Madeleine Mullins?"

"Yes, this is me—I mean, she—I mean, this is Madeleine." She bit her lip.

"I'm so sorry to give you this bad news, but due to the ice storm last night, we will not be able to deliver your food for the wedding today."

"What?" She couldn't think of anything else to say.

"We've lost power to our kitchen and will have to close for the day. Our backup generators are powering the fridges, but we don't have enough gas for those and the ovens."

From the sound of his voice, the man was under even more stress than she was right now.

"Okay, so what does this mean for the money we paid?"

"Under the extreme weather clause of our agreement, we can either reschedule or refund the full amount."

The wedding was still happening today if she had anything to say about the matter.

"We'll take the refund."

"I'm so sorry for the inconvenience."

Inconvenient was having to take a longer route to the church building because a neighbor's tree branch had fallen in the road. This was *way* beyond an inconvenience.

"It's not your fault. Thank you for letting me know."

"We'll refund the full amount once we have power again." He sighed.

Today would be a huge expense for the restaurant. She couldn't be angry at them for the difficulty their power loss caused her.

"Well, we've got another problem." Madeleine raised her voice so everyone could hear her. "The caterers just canceled."

"Are you serious?" Mom's voice rose an octave higher than usual.

"They lost power to the restaurant."

"Wow, that's terrible," Dad said, his voice a bit more sympathetic than Mom's.

"It's out of their control." Madeleine shrugged. "But I don't know what to do about feeding everyone now."

"Let's wait and see how many people can come," Clara said. "I think I have an idea of how we can round up some food."

"Maybe I should call the bakery to check on the cakes." Madeleine held her phone in her hands.

"Let's just focus on making it to the building right now." Dad gave a tight-lipped smile over his shoulder.

"What's that supposed to mean?" Mom kept her eyes on the road, but her threatening tone was directed at Dad.

"Nothing, nothing at all." Dad patted Mom's shoulder, now wincing at Madeleine.

At long last, they pulled up to the church building. Madeleine could tell the parking lot was clearer than the roads they'd traveled to get there.

"Did someone spread salt last night?" she asked nobody in particular.

"Yes," Dad answered. "Sam bought some salt for us to sprinkle around the walkways and parking areas."

"Wow." She'd been in denial that the inclement weather would affect them. She said a silent prayer of thanks for Sam's wisdom.

With the sidewalks and asphalt clear, Madeleine and her family were able to make it to the front doors without much trouble.

"I've got the key." Aunt Clara moved to the front of the pack to unlock the doors.

Madeleine had saved her copy of the key from last summer but was too loaded down with a wedding gown to open the doors herself. How many church members had managed to acquire a copy of the church key?

The air was cold inside the foyer, and Clara made a beeline to the thermostat to turn up the heat. "Let's see if we can get the temperature to above freezing," She laughed, shivering a little.

Dad went back to the car to grab Madeleine's suitcase—a Louisiana honeymoon sounded more wonderful by the minute—

while Madeleine, Mom, and Aunt Clara set up camp in the church nursery. The room offered ample space, dappled sunlight coming through frosted glass windows, and a connecting door to the ladies' restroom.

"I'll give the bakery a call before we get too far along." Madeleine retrieved her phone. "Let's hope they've got power."

"Hello, Green Basket Grocery?" A friendly woman answered the phone.

Madeleine breathed a sigh of relief at the sound of her voice. "Hi, could I have the bakery please?"

"Sure thing."

The phone rang again.

"Green Basket Bakery, this is Wendy."

"Hi, Wendy. This is Madeleine Mullins. I'm calling to check on the cakes for my wedding today."

"Oh, yes, they came out real nice. We'll be bringing those over to you after noon today. Is that time still okay?" Her tone of voice sounded absolutely normal, as if she had no idea there'd been an ice storm.

"That's great. I was just checking because of the storm."

"Oh, sure." Wendy's voice registered recognition as if she'd forgotten about the sheets of frozen water covering the roads. "We're good. You're down on Main Street, right?"

"Yes."

"Don't worry, sweetie. We'll be just fine."

They exchanged pleasant goodbyes, and Madeleine disconnected the call.

"Well? That sounded like good news." Mom watched her, waiting for the verdict.

She blinked.

"Um, yeah. They said they'll be here no problem."

Aunt Clara laughed. "That's what comes from ordering from a local bakery. I knew they'd come through."

So far, exactly one part of this wedding was going according to plan.

36

A.J. groaned in frustration as his alarm rang out. He rolled over to grab his phone, and then it hit him.

Today.

It's today.

A.J. was getting married today.

Better than a shot of espresso, the adrenaline coursing through his body yanked him upright.

He whooped in excitement before remembering that his parents and sisters were sharing his house for the weekend.

Right.

A.J. needed to be at the building before the rest of his family in order to meet with the groomsmen—the ones not taken out by the flu—and Sam.

Picking up his phone again, he saw a text message from Madeleine.

> I'm sorry. I love you. Please forgive me. You were right.

His heart burst at the sight of those words. There she was.

His kind and loving Maddy had been there all along. She'd simply been harder to see the past few weeks.

Below the message from Madeleine was another notification, a weather alert for a winter storm.

He walked to the window, pressing his fingers against the glass. Looked like quite a bit of ice hit Shady Springs the night before. He was thankful he had a reliable pickup truck to get him to the church building safely.

His parents were awake and at the kitchen table already, taking up both of his two chairs. Maybe Madeleine had been right about needing to buy some more furniture. But that was a problem for another day.

"Good morning!" He grinned, bending to squeeze his mom in a hug.

"I hope so. It's looking rough out there." His dad frowned over his mug of coffee. Even though A.J. didn't drink the stuff, he kept a jar of instant granules in the pantry for guests. From the look on Dad's face, it didn't taste as good as what he was used to.

"Stop it, Arthur." Mom waved a hand at him dismissively. "No matter what, it will be a day to remember." She beamed at A.J.

"That's right, Mom. It sure will."

If the salt did its job, the walkways around the church building should be safe. The only problem would be getting everyone to the ceremony. But that wasn't his concern—he merely needed to get himself there. He didn't care a lick who else showed up to watch him marry Madeleine.

"You guys think you'll be okay? I've got cereal in the pantry."

"No milk," his dad grumbled.

"Sorry, I've been a bit busy." A.J. tried his best to sound apologetic. But could the guy give him a break? He'd been busy grading exams, recovering from the flu, and preparing to get married for crying out loud.

"Don't worry about that. We'll be fine." Mom shot daggers at his father before returning her gaze to A.J. "Do you need anything from us? We were planning to get the girls up in about an hour."

"That'll work, depending on how long they take to get ready." If his memory served him correctly, they could spend upwards of two hours primping in the bathroom mirror if given the opportunity.

"I think they'll get dressed and ready at the building with Madeleine," Mom said.

"Great." He poured himself a bowl of dry cereal and grabbed a spoon from the drawer.

"Do you need us to wash dishes for you? So you don't have to come home to a mess after your honeymoon?"

He hadn't thought of that. Madeleine would be coming to his house after the honeymoon. To live. For the first time that day, his nerves kicked in.

"That would be great, Mom. Thank you." He shoveled five more mouthfuls of cereal before placing his bowl in the sink. Then he thought better of it and put the bowl and spoon in the dishwasher. "I'm going to go pack my bags."

Knowing Madeleine, she'd had her honeymoon luggage ready to go for weeks.

A.J. had forgotten he needed to bring stuff with him to the wedding until precisely that moment.

No matter, he wasn't picky about clothes.

He briefly checked the weather for Louisiana before tossing his toiletries bag, three pairs of jeans, five shirts, five pairs of socks and underwear, and five undershirts in his suitcase. A jacket went in. A belt. Sweatpants for sleeping.

I should probably bring one nice outfit.

Slacks, a collared shirt, dress socks, and brown loafers joined the rest of the contents of the suitcase.

Satisfied, A.J. zipped up his bag and set it by the door.

His suit for the wedding was already hanging in a garment bag in his closet, ready to go. He only needed socks and shoes.

Done.

A.J. shrugged. That had been even easier than he'd thought it would be.

Now to get to the church building.

37

He'd forgotten how low the gas gauge was yesterday. When A.J. turned the key in the ignition, the needle twitched a hair above "E" and stopped completely.

He groaned.

The day before, he'd been so preoccupied with his argument with Madeleine, he'd neglected to swing by the gas station on his way home from the church building. And now it was the day of the wedding.

There was no way he'd make it out of town with his bride if he didn't fill up right now. But could he make it to the station?

He'd never been a plan-ahead kind of person with a full extra tank at the ready in his garage. The red can he kept for mowing lawns in the summer sat empty on the shelf.

The only way to make it to the building was to inch his way down the street and pray for the best.

Lord, please let me make it to the gas station.

He put the truck in reverse and slowly backed out of the driveway and around his parents' car.

The trees on either side of his street bent under the weight of the ice covering their branches. An untouched sheet of ice covered the road. No one else had been crazy enough to venture out in this weather. He rolled over the ice at a glacial speed, keeping his hands tight on the wheel.

Pushing the acceleration pedal only when absolutely necessary, A.J. made it out of his neighborhood and onto the highway. If he could drive two miles down the road, he'd be at the closest gas station. It wasn't the cheapest place in town, but it would work.

Half a mile in, the needle of the gas gauge bounced down below the "E."

Come on, come on.

The truck kept rolling another second on the highway.

Two more seconds.

Almost there.

Then, it sputtered and died.

A.J. had exactly enough momentum to pull over to the shoulder. Not that it mattered. There weren't any other drivers out on the road.

The only thing to do was walk. He hopped out of the truck and shut the door, only then remembering the empty gas can on the shelf in his garage. Would've been nice to have that to carry the gas back to the truck.

Sighing, A.J. shoved his gloved hands in the pockets of his coat, and marched off in the direction of the gas station, stepping carefully on the ice until he could walk in the grass on the side of the road.

The morning was quiet and calm, except for a high-pitched shrieking wind that blew in his ears. A.J. pulled the hood of his coat over his head. He breathed in the icy air. What a way to start his wedding day.

When A.J. heard another truck inching down the highway, he gasped. Turning suddenly, he waved his arms above his head.

"Hey, over here. Help!"

Likely, the sight of a person was just as alarming to the driver of the truck as the sight of the vehicle had been to A.J. The driver slowed to a crawl and stopped beside him.

A.J. smiled when the window began rolling down, but his grin grew enormous when he saw who was inside.

"Need a ride?" Sam Sullivan poked his head out of the passenger side, and directly behind him in the driver's seat was John Patterson.

"I sure do." Relief flooded his chest. "I ran out of gas."

"Come on in. We'll help you get to the station and back to your truck."

A.J. pulled open the door and stepped onto the running board. Sam scooted over, making enough room for him to squeeze in.

Mr. Patterson's truck was much nicer than A.J.'s. It smelled of leather and polish. A whoosh of hot air blew from the vents. A.J. was sure Mr. Patterson wouldn't be caught with any less than half a tank of gas in *his* truck.

True to his word, Mr. Patterson got A.J. to the station and even lent him his empty gas can to fill up.

"Rough weather out there, huh?" The man behind the counter whistled, shaking his head as he rang up A.J.'s bill on the cash register.

"I'm getting married today." He didn't know why he shared that information with the cashier.

The man snorted a laugh. "Congratulations. I hope it's a beautiful wedding."

"It'll be perfect."

And he knew it would be. If only he could actually make it to the wedding.

38

$\mathcal{M}$adeleine paced the long foyer, clutching her coat around her shoulders. At each end of the hallway, she pressed her hands against the glass doors, searching for A.J. Then she'd turn around, walk to the doors on the other end, and do the same thing, straining her eyes for a glimpse of his vehicle.

Every once in a while, a truck would slowly roll down the highway in front of the building, but they never turned into the church parking lot.

Right now, she should be getting ready for her wedding. Surrounded by her bridesmaids, mother, and mother-in-law. Taking photos of her ring or shoes or veil. She should be hiding from her future husband, worried about superstitions.

But none of that mattered. She needed to see him.

Mom walked through the double doors of the auditorium. "You still haven't heard anything from A.J.?" She winced.

"No."

Dad joined them from the small classroom where he'd camped out with his camera and equipment. "I've got everything ready to go, as soon as—"

Mom cut him off with a sharp shake of her head.

"Still no word from A.J.?" he asked.

Madeleine shook her head. Her eyes stung, and she pressed her fingers to the inside corners of her eyes, looking to the ceiling to avoid smudging her mascara.

She'd put on makeup but couldn't bear to change into her dress yet. What if it was all for nothing?

Why hadn't he answered her text last night? Had her last outburst been enough to change his mind? Was she going to live the rest of her life alone, a jilted bride?

"Come here. Let's sit down while we wait." Mom gently tugged on Madeleine's arm, still bundled under the coat, and led her to a pew at the back of the auditorium.

In the dimmed lights, everything was gorgeous.

The electric candles looked authentic from a distance. The poinsettias and foraged evergreen branches added a rustic charm. The velvet ribbon bows and sprigs of cedar and juniper on the inside ends of the pews added precisely the right amount of color. The scene looked like a picture from a magazine.

"Oh, Mom." Madeleine's voice cracked.

"What is it, sweetie?" Mom wrapped her arms around Madeleine, worry written all across her face. "Do you not like the decorations? I can change them."

"No, you did a wonderful job. I love it."

They'd actually pulled it off. Despite illness and mishaps— and fire!—they'd crafted a beautiful wedding. The invitations were perfectly designed (if a little late), the bridesmaids and groomsmen had attractive outfits (even if most of them were sick), and the cake was sure to be delicious (assuming the bakers made it to the church building). Okay, maybe it wasn't a perfect, beautiful wedding.

But she'd done the best she could, and God would provide the rest. Right?

"But it's not going to happen, is it?" Madeleine sat in the

pew and leaned forward, resting her head in her hands. "He's not coming."

"Of course, he'll be here. It's his wedding day."

"No, I forgot the whole point." She tilted her weight to the side, leaning against her mother.

Mom rubbed Madeleine's shoulder, not saying anything yet, but offering her comforting presence.

"None of this matters without him." Madeleine gestured around the room. "I don't need any of it, the fancy decorations, the food." She barked a laugh. "I don't even need any of the people."

Madeleine pressed her eyes shut. "I just need A.J."

"Hey! I think I see someone," Dad called out from the front hall.

Madeleine and her mother raced out to join him by the doors.

A large black truck slowly rumbled through the icy parking lot and pulled up to the awning. When the truck stopped, a door opened on the other side and Sam Sullivan got out.

Madeleine's heart dropped.

It wasn't A.J. He wasn't coming.

A short, burly man, bundled up in a black coat and gloves stepped into the foyer, taking off his wool beanie. Mr. Patterson.

And right behind him, Sam.

"Hi, Sam. Hi, Mr. Patterson." Madeleine couldn't quite keep the worry out of her voice.

"Come and get warm." Aunt Clara pulled Sam inside.

"I've got a couple more trips to make, but I think we can still pull off a wedding." Mr. Patterson looked at Madeleine. "If you don't mind waiting a little while."

"Not at all." She gave him a cautious smile, not having the heart to tell him the wedding couldn't happen until the groom showed up.

Mr. Patterson nodded goodbye and headed back out into the cold.

"John called out of the blue this morning and offered to pick me up. I didn't mind not having to drive in this weather." Sam pulled his coat off. "And then, who should we run into, but—"

Another pickup truck pulled under the awning.

Madeleine spotted a flash of red hair. She sucked in a breath.

A.J. raced around the front of the truck and crashed into the building, into Madeleine's arms.

She couldn't help it anymore. The tears streamed freely down her face. She stared into those gorgeous green eyes and pulled him in for a kiss. Wrapping his arms around her waist, A.J. returned her affection with gusto.

"I thought you weren't coming." She spoke against his shoulder as she squeezed him in a hug.

A.J. pulled back quickly, his brow furrowed in shock. "Of course, I came. It's our wedding day."

"But last night."

He stopped her by pressing his fingers to her lips. "Last night we were all under a lot of stress. We all said things we didn't mean. But I'm in this for life, Madeleine Mullins." He kissed her again, this time on her forehead. "Now that doesn't mean I almost didn't make it here."

"As I was saying," Sam said, turning to Clara. "We found A.J. on the side of the highway, walking to the gas station."

"What?" Mom interrupted.

"I got kind of busy and forgot to fill up last night." A.J. shrugged sheepishly.

Madeleine couldn't be mad. Her soon-to-be-husband was here and she was getting married. "In a matter of minutes, you turned the worst day to the best day, just by walking in those doors." She gripped his forearm with her left hand and ran the fingers of her right hand through his hair, stroking his temple with her thumb. "I went about everything the wrong way. The only thing that matters about today is that I get to marry the man of my dreams. I love you so much."

"I love you too. You look beautiful, by the way." He pulled back to look her over.

"Okay, I know you've already seen the bride, but let's pretend like that never happened." Mom tugged Madeleine away, while Dad came to stand beside A.J. "We'll be over here if you need us."

Madeleine allowed herself to be whisked away to the nursery, content to do whatever Mom had in mind (probably fix her ruined makeup). What did it matter, as long as she got to marry A.J. at the end of it?

39

Madeleine's perfect wedding ended up not being like a fairy tale after all. John Patterson and other volunteers with sturdy vehicles spent all morning and part of the afternoon trekking north and south, east and west in their trucks, gathering people for Madeleine and A.J.'s wedding. After a few hours of rounding up family and friends, only about three dozen people sat in the pews of the auditorium.

Several family members FaceTimed in from their homes or hotels in Fayetteville. Older guests or those with young children chose to stay put rather than risk a car accident on the ice.

Stepping out from behind a partition in the church nursery, Madeleine twirled in her dress. "How do I look?"

Delicate ivory lace covered her bodice and trailed down her arms in long sleeves. A modest sweetheart neckline flowed into a fitted waist. Pearl buttons ran the length of her back. The A-line skirt was just full enough to balance the dress without distracting from the details of her bodice and sleeves.

"You look stunning," Felicity breathed.

"Wow, Madeleine," Olivia said. "I think you might make A.J. cry, you're so beautiful."

The girls giggled, walking nearer to squeeze Madeleine's hands and admire her dress up close.

Mom sighed behind her. They'd spent the last few hours curling and pinning hair, touching up her makeup, and performing the delicate procedure of getting into the wedding dress.

Madeleine stared at herself in the full-length mirror propped up in the corner of the room.

It had all been worth it.

"It's time for you girls to get into the foyer." Clara—the unofficial wedding coordinator—poked her head in the door to call for Felicity and Olivia. She froze when she saw Madeleine. "Oh, honey. You look so beautiful."

"Thanks, Aunt Clara."

Clara tightened her lips, waving her hands frantically. "Don't cry, don't cry." She ducked back out of the room.

"Should I go get Dad to walk you down the aisle?" Mom didn't wait to hear Madeleine's response, leaving her alone in the nursery.

Madeleine found a plastic chair and fluffed her skirt over the back of it, sitting gently. She couldn't touch her face or her hair, so she perched on the chair and thought.

God had carried her and A.J. to this moment. Although the journey was painful, God had been faithful to them. All of the times she'd wondered if He was trying to prevent their marriage, He was guiding them. God hadn't been closing doors. He'd been shaping Madeleine's heart to see what truly mattered.

Just like Mom had said that morning, she needed to keep the important things important. Honoring God by loving A.J. would give her a great marriage, not a fabulous wedding.

She breathed—as deeply as she could in the tight dress—and closed her eyes while she waited.

"Hey, sweetie. Are you ready?" Dad and Mom stood in the doorway.

"Yes, I'm ready."

* * *

When the last of the expected guests had arrived, and Shelby had settled in at the laptop in the back of the auditorium, the strains of classical music floated over the hushed crowd. None of the grandparents had ventured out. Only A.J.'s parents walked down the aisle to the music.

Someone peeked through a window in the doors at the back of the auditorium, but in a flash they were gone. A.J. couldn't say for sure, but it looked like Madeleine's face.

Deep breath.

The music changed and Felicity and Olivia each made their way up the aisle, walking to their assigned spots on the stage.

Then the back doors opened, and everyone stood.

Madeleine walked into sight—with both of her parents. Henry stood at her right and Catherine at her left. They each wrapped a hand through one of her arms.

Gentle music played as she stepped slowly toward him.

A.J.'s breath caught in his throat.

She was the most exquisite sight, as radiant as snow in her dress.

He knew she'd ask him later about how everything looked, but all he could see was Madeleine's face. And she smiled back at him. Joy filled her eyes and brightened her cheeks.

In no time at all, she was in front of him.

Sam welcomed the crowd.

"Who gives this woman to be married?" he asked.

"We do." Henry and Catherine spoke in unison. They took turns kissing Madeleine on her cheeks.

When Henry wiped his eyes, A.J. felt his own stinging. He blinked quickly. He didn't mind crying, but he didn't want to miss a second.

Sam tucked his Bible under his arm, took both of their hands, and led them in prayer. He asked God to bless their marriage and thanked Him for bringing everyone safely together today.

Sam squeezed their hands again, then gave them to each other. He invited the audience to be seated.

Stroking the soft skin of her hand with his thumb, a feeling of peace mingled with A.J.'s excitement. This was exactly where he was meant to be.

When he spoke again, Sam reminded them of the story of Christmas. And the larger story of the Bible.

"God has pursued us for as long as man has existed. He loved us so much that He came down to Earth to be among us.

"In marriage, God gives us a living model of His love for us. Your relationship will be challenging. Even more challenging than pulling together this wedding."

Everyone laughed, even Madeleine.

"But God will bless and reward your effort."

Staring into the eyes of his bride, A.J.'s heart swelled. He could imagine the years of life before them. Some challenging, some happy, all of them blessed by God.

"A.J.—I mean, Arthur—" Sam turned a bright red.

"A.J. is fine," he whispered. No sense in switching his name just to be formal.

"A.J., do you take Madeleine to be your lawfully wedded wife? To love, honor, and cherish for better or worse, for richer or for poorer, in sickness and in health, until death do you part?" Sam continued with the vows.

"I do."

Sam repeated the vows for Madeleine.

Her voice wavered with emotion, but Madeleine repeated the words, "I do."

"Do you have the rings?"

Cole held up Madeleine's ring, and Olivia produced his.

A.J. let out a breath he hadn't realized he'd been holding.

"With this ring, I thee wed."

One by one, they repeated a pledge to each other. To honor and love each other and God, and to keep Him first in their marriage.

When Madeleine slipped the ring on his finger, the sensation was strange at first. He'd never worn jewelry before and now he'd be wearing this ring for the rest of his life. But he didn't mind learning to get used to the feeling.

"And now." Sam turned to the people sitting in the pews. "Do you, their friends and family, pledge to do everything in your power to support Madeleine and A.J. in their marriage and to encourage them to follow God and love each other?"

A.J. raised his brow in surprise. He'd never heard the officiant ask the crowd to say a vow before, but he liked it.

"We do."

Looking out to the people surrounding them, A.J. smiled. Absolutely everyone there had made some sort of a sacrifice to attend their wedding that day. They'd already proven their love and dedication to Madeleine and him. He knew they'd keep their end of the deal.

"A.J. and Madeleine, having proclaimed your love and commitment to each other in the sight of God and these witnesses, it is my absolute delight, by the power vested in me by the state of Arkansas and—most importantly—by God, I now pronounce you husband and wife."

He grinned at A.J. "You may kiss the bride."

Finally.

Taking Madeleine's face in his hands, he gently tugged her toward him. He pressed his lips to hers and felt her sigh against him.

A cheer rang out among the crowd.

After a respectable three seconds, A.J. pulled away. They'd save the real kissing for later.

"Ladies and gentlemen, I present to you, Mr. and Mrs. Young!"

40

Madeleine tugged A.J. into a classroom outside the foyer and pushed the door shut behind them. "We did it. We actually got married." She reached her hands up to his face, pulling him down for a kiss.

He groaned, returning her kiss with passion. "I almost can't believe it."

Knock, knock.

They pulled apart quickly as if doing something wrong when Cole, Matt, Felicity, and Olivia walked in the room.

"Your dad said he wants us to wait here with the family while guests go to the reception so we can snap some pictures."

"Right." Madeleine wiped her lips sheepishly.

A.J. laced his fingers through hers.

Their parents and extended family joined them and soon the classroom was quite full.

"Okay, everyone," Dad called out. "Let's all go have a seat in the auditorium. We'll start with the Young side of the family on the stage."

They all smiled and posed obediently while Dad and his assistant Leah took pictures of A.J.'s family and Madeleine's

229

family. Then the wedding party had their turn, and finally, just A.J. and Madeleine.

"Can we be done now?" Madeleine asked through her teeth, smiling into A.J.'s eyes while Dad took his billionth photo.

"Okay, okay," Dad relented petulantly. "Sorry if I wanted you to have happy memories of your wedding day."

Madeleine laughed. "I don't think anyone will be forgetting this wedding anytime soon."

When Madeleine walked into the fellowship hall, A.J. on her arm, she squealed in delight.

True to their word, the Green Basket Bakery delivered the cakes on time. A beautiful tiered white wedding cake with buttercream frosting flowers and glittery sugar rested on a table, drawing everyone's attention when they first walked into the reception. Beside it, a chocolate sheet cake promised to be equally delicious.

Unbeknownst to Madeleine and A.J., several members of the church had brought food to share. And Aunt Clara had added fruit and platters of meat and cheese to their order from Green Basket Grocery. Somehow, there was more than enough food for everyone. The spread of dishes looked a little more like a potluck than an organized, catered meal, but who didn't love a church potluck?

Sam spotted the happy couple walking through the double doors of the fellowship hall and stood. "Mr. and Mrs. Young, everybody!"

The nearly forty people in the room clapped and cheered like four hundred. Shelby found A.J.'s laptop plugged into the speaker system and turned on their reception playlist.

"How about you go through the line and get some food? We've got the photographer all night." Aunt Clara winked at them, handing them each a plate.

Because the caterer hadn't come, there were no china plates. Only paper ones from the pantry. But at least they were the fancy heavyweight kind. And someone had found silver-looking plastic cutlery.

"I'd always heard brides and grooms complain about not being able to eat anything at their weddings, but I have a feeling we'll be just fine." Madeleine scooped macaroni and cheese and sliced strawberries on her plate.

"Maybe all weddings should be more like ours." A.J. laughed.

There was something to be said for the laid-back nature of their wedding reception. Everyone had a chance to visit with Madeleine and A.J. *and* eat their fill, and no one mentioned the missing guest favors. The cake was plenty big for everyone to have seconds and save the top tier for the newlyweds.

"Why do we need the top of the cake?" A.J. asked as he watched his mom set it aside in a box.

"It's for your first anniversary," Ginger said. "You can freeze it until you're ready to eat it."

"We'll see if it still tastes any good after a year in a freezer and a move to Sayers." Madeleine shrugged.

"Do you have a minute?" Sam tugged Madeleine's elbow. "We have one last thing we need to do."

Dad followed them back to the older section of the building and into Sam's office. "You're not official in the eyes of the state of Arkansas until you sign this license."

"Oh, right." Madeleine had forgotten about the paperwork. "I figured we were already official."

Sam handed her a pen for her to sign her name and pointed to the correct line. Then A.J. had his turn.

"Now you're completely and totally official." Sam handed the license over to them.

"How about we let Mom hang onto this for now?" Dad asked.

"Not a bad idea," Madeleine agreed. She had a party to get back to.

* * *

A.J. chatted with everyone at the reception. He ate some dinner and a slice of each kind of cake. He personally thanked John Patterson multiple times for saving the day.

But it was time to leave.

Madeleine was visiting with Nancy Jones, holding one of her hands in hers.

He sidled up to her and slid a stray lock of hair behind her ear. Leaning close, he whispered. "Are you ready?"

Madeleine shivered and gazed up at him. "Ready for what?" she whispered back.

He raised an eyebrow.

"Oh, right." Her cheeks burned a bright red.

Nancy giggled. "Is it time for you two to head out of here?"

Nodding, A.J. tugged her away. "You've thrown the bouquet, I tossed the garter, we've eaten and talked …" What was left to do? "Do you have your bags packed?"

"Yes, but I'd like to change before we leave."

He swept his hand out, gesturing to their outfits. "You don't want to check into our hotel in a wedding dress?"

"No." She gathered the side of her dress with one hand in a curtsy. "Not particularly."

"All right then. I'll load up the suitcases."

Loosening his tie and unbuttoning the first button of his shirt was all it took to change from formal to dressy-casual. A.J. retrieved his coat and hat from the classroom where he'd stashed his suitcase and rolled it down the hall to the exit.

"Going so soon?" His dad jogged down the hall, catching up.

"We'll say our big goodbyes before we leave. I'm just loading up the truck."

"Need any help?"

He didn't, but A.J. shrugged. "Sure. You can take this and I'll grab Madeleine's bags."

After stopping by the nursery where Madeleine had set her suitcases outside the door, A.J. joined up with his dad.

"You two pulled off a pretty decent wedding." Dad nodded at him over his shoulder.

"It wasn't easy, but we had a lot of help."

Dad tossed A.J.'s suitcase in the bed, and A.J. did the same with Madeleine's bags. Then he covered them all with a tarp and strapped it down.

"I'm proud of you, son." Dad clapped him on the shoulder. "I know you don't need it, but I'd like to add a little more to your honeymoon fund." He slipped a wad of cash into A.J.'s palm.

"Thanks, Dad." What was this about?

"You were right, what you said at Thanksgiving. You've been managing on your own just fine the last few years." He shrugged. "Maybe you can use it for moving expenses—take Madeleine out for a nice dinner—you can decide, whatever you like."

A.J. could tell it pained his dad to think about spending money on something as frivolous as dinner. "I'm sure Madeleine would be happy to put it toward something practical. Thanks, Dad."

"You're welcome." He nodded and took a couple steps forward before looking over his shoulder. "Have a good trip."

A.J. caught up to him and pulled him into a hug. "Thank you." He gripped his father tight until he could feel him relax into the embrace. Before it could get too awkward, he pulled back, patted him once on the shoulder, and left to find his wife.

"Mrs. Young? Are you ready?" A.J. tapped on the nursery door.

The knob turned and Madeleine stepped out.

When would he stop being amazed every time he saw her?

She wore a long-sleeved dress, an emerald green that looked right at home with all of the Christmas decorations around them. It reached down to her calves, where A.J. could see she'd chosen to wear boots—a good choice in this weather. Her hair still hung in loose curls around her shoulders.

He cleared his throat. "Um, are you …?"

"Yes." She reached out for his hand.

When she walked out of the doorway, A.J. turned to see their family had gathered around. They must've noticed the newlyweds were missing from the reception.

Catherine was the first to step forward. "I love you." She flung her arms around her daughter. "I'm so proud of you. You did such a great job pulling off this wedding."

"You all did most of the work." Madeleine's gaze roamed around the hall to all the people surrounding them.

"No." Henry took his turn hugging his daughter, giving Catherine a chance to dab at her eyes with a tissue. Just low enough that only Madeleine and A.J. could hear, he said, "I love you, Maddy-Maddy-Bo-Baddy."

"I love you, too, Daddy-Daddy-Bo-Baddy." Madeleine giggled.

"Bye, drive safe." Felicity and Olivia hugged him and Madeleine in turn.

"I love you, sweetie." Mom squeezed him around his middle. "I'm so proud of you."

A.J. had already said goodbye to his dad earlier and wasn't expecting anything more, but Arthur Senior stepped in quietly and gave him one last, unexpected hug.

"I guess we'd better let everyone else know to wave goodbye." Aunt Clara flung her arm around her niece and led her to the fellowship hall where the rest of their family and friends were.

Walking as quickly as they could through a tunnel of well-wishers, A.J. and Madeleine headed out the door to his truck.

It wasn't quite the dramatic getaway he'd like. Instead of peeling out of the parking lot, he had to wait for the engine to warm up and then crawl away cautiously.

Madeleine rolled down the window and waved to the people brave enough to gather in the cold. She called out *goodbyes* to them until they couldn't see the church building anymore.

"What should we do next?" A.J. asked, unable to keep the laughter from his voice, and barely able to keep from staring at his bride.

"I don't care." Madeleine grinned at him. "As long as I get to do it with you."

The End

DISCUSSION QUESTIONS

1. What is your favorite part of a wedding? What's your least favorite—and why?
2. Madeleine faces a series of disasters during wedding planning. Do you have any funny or memorable wedding mishaps to share?
3. A.J. and Madeleine go through premarital counseling with Sam Sullivan. Do you think premarital counseling is necessary? What's one question every couple should ask before getting married?
4. How does faith play a key role in A.J. and Madeleine's journey? How do they each grow spiritually over the course of the story?
5. What did you think about A.J. and Madeleine's relationship dynamic? In what ways do they complement or challenge each other?
6. This story contrasts Madeleine's desire for a "perfect" wedding with God's plan for something better. Have you ever had a time when God redefined your expectations?

7. Would you ever plan a December wedding? Why or why not?

8. Which Bible verse or spiritual theme stood out to you most while reading the book?

9. How might this story inspire you to reframe expectations or pursue peace in your own life?

10. What's your favorite fictional wedding from a book or movie?

ACKNOWLEDGMENTS

I will never tire of thanking Amy R. Anguish—my dear friend, mentor, accountability partner, and now editor. You are a rockstar. I've learned so much from your wisdom and relentless encouragement. I love you!

Thank you to Kathy McKinsey, Heather Greer, Linda Fulkerson, Liana George, and everyone at Scrivenings Press. I'm so blessed to be able to work with such a kind, Christ-centered team.

There are several people I must acknowledge for their part in contributing real-life wedding stories to this book. Uncle Mark and Aunt Kim, John and Mallory, and Heather. I pray God would continue to richly bless all of the real marriages represented in this fictional work.

Thank you to Jessica Uranga, my mom Rebecca Vinzant, and all of the precious women at Beautiful Lives in Northwest Arkansas. I'm honored to share your ministry with my readers.

To those of us who planned weddings before Pinterest or Instagram—I salute you. And to those dear sweet babies who have to plan a wedding in the age of high-resolution internet scrutiny, you are brave and beautiful. May we all remember that weddings are just one day. Marriage is the masterpiece.

Let us never forget who is truly in charge—and what matters most. Thank you, Lord, for loving us even in our forgetfulness.

ABOUT SARAH ANNE CROUCH

Sarah Anne Crouch aims to bless readers with inspirational fiction brimming with heart.

The author of *A Summer in Shady Springs*, *A Homecoming in Shady Springs*, "A Sweet Dream Come True" from the *Love in Any Season* collection, and "Where Love is Planted" from the *Love Delivered* collection, Sarah writes stories featuring characters growing in love and their relationships with God.

Although Sarah always wanted to be an author, she spent time as a fifth-grade English teacher, earned a degree in library science, and currently makes feeble attempts to corral her children as a stay-at-home mom.

Sarah has lived in many places but calls Arkansas home and draws inspiration from the beautiful surroundings of the Natural State. A graduate of Harding University, she remains actively involved with her alma mater.

Outside of writing, Sarah enjoys reading books, exploring recipes, playing piano music, and cherishing emails from her readers.

A Summer in Shady Springs

Book One of the Shady Springs Series

The last place Madeleine Mullins wants to be is back in Shady Springs, Arkansas—the town where her whole world fell apart. But when her beloved Aunt Clara begs her for help, Madeleine reluctantly takes a job painting a mural at her aunt's church. Her plan is to finish quickly and leave her bad memories behind. But the more time she spends with the handsome youth minister and the more she reads her Bible, the more she wonders if she has been wrong about God and the Church all along.

Three years out of college, and A.J. Young still doesn't know what he wants to be when he grows up. He knows he wants to settle down and build a family but hasn't found the wife he'd like to share his life with. Then Madeleine comes to town. Their friendship buds quickly, although it can never be anything more as long as she isn't a Christian.

An undeniable attraction grows between A.J. and Madeleine, but she's only in town for a few weeks, and he can't date someone who doesn't share his beliefs. How can Madeleine help A.J. discover a passion for the career he's always wanted?

Get your copy here:

https://scrivenings.link/asummerinshadysprings

* * *

A Homecoming in Shady Springs

Book Two of the Shady Springs Series

Catherine and Henry Mullins never thought they'd see each other again after their traumatic separation, but the engagement of their only daughter forces them together. As they spend time focusing on the wedding, Catherine realizes how much she still loves Henry. But is it too late for one more chance?

Twenty-five years earlier, Henry meets Cate on the campus of Halloway

University. Although Cate makes it abundantly clear she isn't interested in a romantic relationship, Henry can't seem to resist her. Can he convince her to give him a shot? And will their love survive tragedy?

Follow Henry and Catherine as they journey through love over the years and discover that life is better with someone by your side.

Get your copy here:

https://scrivenings.link/ahomecominginshadysprings

A Match Made at Christmas

A novella collection—includes "A Match of Her Own"

by Sarah Anne Crouch

***A-parent-ly Christmas* (by Amy R Anguish)**—Noel and Joy Davidson didn't mean to separate, but a job promotion and educational opportunities were too much for their marriage to withstand. Now, it's Christmas and their son Andy wants them together. Between his mischief, an unexpected snowstorm, and the holiday spirit, they're remembering why they first wanted to be together. But which one will give up their dream for the other?

***A Match of her Own* (by Sarah Anne Crouch)**—Victoria Wood is torn between elation and devastation now that her sister is married and gone. When she realizes her sister's best friend is alone and best-friend-less on Christmas, she knows just what to do. Set her up with a boyfriend! But pesky Jared Knight keeps getting in the way. Jared can't date Victoria— she's too immature—but he can't convince his heart to move on. How will he keep Victoria from ruining everyone's love lives? When will she realize her perfect match is closer than she thinks?

***Jingle Bell Matchmakers* (by Lori DeJong)**—When country music star Aubrey Mayfield is lured home after years away, she's bewildered when she and ex-fiance-now-widowed-dad Cody Lansdale keep finding themselves in the same place at the same time. As they become reacquainted, however, old feelings stir. Aubrey's at a crossroads in her career and is contemplating a change. But when a chance at headlining her own tour takes her back to Nashville, Cody realizes her dreams may once again come between them. Unless God, with a little help from the Jingle Bell Committee, has a better plan.

***The Santa Setup* (by Heather Greer)**—Turning friendship into love takes magic. Good thing Nicholas Eckert and Julie Clarke work at Christmas Wonderland. The attraction brims with holiday magic, not to mention four teenage elves determined that Mr. and Mrs. Claus stop playing a couple and become one. The teens will need more than mistletoe to pair up these two. Julie is seeing someone, and Nick won't risk their friendship for possible love. Only the elven employees' outrageous antics stand a chance of setting up Santa in time for Christmas.

Get your copy here:

https://scrivenings.link/amatchmadeatchristmas

* * *

Love Delivered

A novella collection—includes "Where Love Is Planted"

by Sarah Anne Crouch

***Romance at Register Five* (by Amy R Anguish)**—Mack McDonald isn't happy about the Grocerease app coming to his grocery store. But he's committed to the sixty-day trial period, and braces himself to lose money. Kaitlyn Daniels loves how the Grocerease app helps her make ends meet so she can assist her mom, the reason she moved to small Sassafras, AR. Mack and Kaitlyn struggle to overcome differing opinions on the perks of the app. But if they don't, it could keep them from something even better.

***Where Love is Planted* (by Sarah Anne Crouch)**—Ivy Aaronson is surrounded by family at their flower shop in West Texas—just the way she likes it. But she's given up hope on ever finding a man who understands her choices. When attorney Grant Keller orders flowers for his mother, Ivy wonders if maybe there are indeed some considerate men left in the world…until she finds out Grant's relationship with his parents is less than ideal. How can Ivy ever find love when every man she meets puts career over family?

***Sweet Delivery* (by Heather Greer)**—After winning Cake That, Will Forrester thinks his Pastry Perfect Baking Dreams have come true. The sweetness fades when a chain bakery moves to town, and Will must adjust his plans to keep his customers. Hiring Erica Gerard is one of those changes. As they work together, Erica challenges Will and offers new ideas to improve the bakery. Soon, Erica and Will start bringing out the best in each other. But Erica harbors a secret, and if it's discovered, Will might never be the same.

***The Mermaids, the Ex, and USSS* (by Rachel Herod)**—Braig Sanborn is the most loyal employee the United States Shipping Service has ever seen, which is why he agreed to transfer across the country with only a few weeks' notice. Bailey Bivens is so busy planning a friend's wedding, she didn't expect to fall for the carrier who delivers packages to her house. When they both find themselves in too deep, will they agree the relationship was doomed from the start?

Get your copy here:

https://scrivenings.link/lovedelivered

* * *

Love in Any Season

A novella collection—includes "A Sweet Dream Come True"

by Sarah Anne Crouch

Spring Has Sprung(by **Regina Rudd Merrick**)—Laurel Pascal, Assistant City Manager of Spring, Kentucky, is tasked with organizing the town's beloved Daffodil Festival, and she's not happy. An allergy sufferer all her life, she dreads the season from the first Daffodil bloom in the yard to the last coat of pollen on her car. Newcomer Dr. Owen Roswell volunteers to help, and soon finds that not only does Laurel need his expertise as an allergist, but help in appreciating the season she's obligated to celebrate.

What does he want more—for Laurel to fall in love with his favorite season? Or him?

The Missing Piece (by **Amy R. Anguish**)—Beth Norton and Tommy England grew up together with best-friend moms who had a love of quilting and a business celebrating the craft. When high school ended, though, so did Beth and Tommy's friendship.

When Tommy moves back after seven years and his mother's death, he can't understand why Beth is so angry with him. Helping Beth and her mother stabilize the finances of the business, they're forced to work together. As Tommy sorts through his mother's things, he finds an unfinished quilt, and it turns into a joint project.

With each stitch taken, they work toward more than just a completed blanket.

A Sweet Dream Come True (by **Sarah Anne Crouch**)—Isaac Campbell is living his dream of running an ice cream shop but fears he won't last past the first difficult year. Mel Wilson is a busy single mother who longs to be a chocolatier but is too afraid to turn her dreams into reality.

When Mel and Isaac meet at Bestwood, Tennessee's fall festival, it seems like divine providence. But once Mel agrees to help Isaac bring in customers by selling her chocolates at his shop, she realizes how challenging running a business can be.

Can Mel and Isaac trust in God's provision and make a leap of faith?

Will their partnership end in disaster, or will it be a sweet dream come true?

Sugar and Spice **(by Heather Greer)**—Emeline Becker, owner of Sugar and Spice Bakery, loves New Kuchenbrünn, except for the gingerbread. As the only bakery, she supplies the annual Gingerbread Festival with the one treat she can't stand. It's gingerbread everywhere.

Things get worse when Ryker Lehmann is hired as the festival photographer. He was her secret teen crush, her sister's boyfriend, and witness to her worst humiliation. Plus, he broke her sister's heart and bruised hers when he left town after graduation. Now, he's back in town, determined to fix their friendship before the festival ends.

With gingerbread and Ryker together, can Emmie make it through the festival with her mind and heart intact?

Get your copy here:

https://scrivenings.link/loveinanyseason

Stay up-to-date on your favorite books and authors with our free e-newsletters.

ScriveningsPress.com